HIS CHRISTMAS MIRACLE

A Curvy Girl Holiday Romance

NICHOLE ROSE

NICHOLE ROSE

CONTENTS

DEDICATION

This is for those who believe in the magic of Christmas so fiercely you make everyone around you believe too.

ABOUT THE BOOK

To mend her boss's heart, this teacher will risk her own.

Sawyer

A football game and a cold one was my Christmas plan.

Until Lana Winters swept in and took over.

Spending the holiday with this cheery little elf is all too appealing.

She's the only person alive who makes the guilt lie quietly.

I swore I would never forgive myself for what I caused.

But when she turns those bright eyes on me...all I feel is peace.

She's my miracle, and I'm not letting her go.

Lana

Sawyer Greenway's family is broken. I think he might be too.

Letting him spend Christmas alone would be cruel.

Falling for him would be insane.

But my heart never listens to my head.

When he smiles at me, all I feel is love.

I can't heal his family, but I *will* heal his heart.

Even if doing so means risking my own.

Warning

When this older man meets his curvy younger woman, he has no idea what sort of healing magic is in store for him. If holiday romance, determined heroines, and over-the-top men make your heart happy, you will love Lana and Sawyer's story. This sweet, steamy romance from Nichole Rose comes complete with a sticky-sweet and guaranteed HEA.

CHAPTER ONE

SAWYER

"I wish you would come home for Christmas, Sawyer."

The pout in my baby sister's voice makes my heart twist as regret rushes through me. Savannah is seventeen and sweet as can be. Christmas is magical to her, the one time of year she can get away with spoiling everyone she knows with all the love and affection in her heart.

God knows, she has a lot of it. She's never met a person she couldn't win over with her wide eyes and innocent laughter. I was nineteen when she was born, and she's had me wrapped around her finger ever since. I miss her like crazy and I hate letting her down but going home for the holidays this year isn't an option.

I just accepted a position in San Francisco as the new principal at Commodore Elementary. Finding a house and moving across the state has been a time-consuming venture...and I don't have a whole lot of that available at the moment. Unpacking is going to take me weeks.

The new term starts right after the New Year and I need to hit the ground running. The last principal here was a complete dick from what I understand. He terrorized the staff and the students. Building trust is going to take a lot of work.

I'm more than willing to put in the effort. The Superintendent and his wife—Sebastian and Rowan Thorne—sold me on Commodore as soon as I met them. I want to do right by the teachers and students here and fix what Richard Johnson broke. They deserve a principal who cares about their well-being. I think I'm the man for the job. I just need to prove it to them.

Even if I had time to fly home to San Bernardino, I can't. Saint, my younger brother, is home for the holidays. Last time we were home at the same time, things didn't end well. Saint is difficult. He's half a decade younger than I am, and reckless as hell. He's a big deal in the music industry, a certified rock god. Somewhere along the way, he bought into all the hype.

The night before Thanksgiving last year, he almost killed Savannah after rolling his car with her inside. It was storming and he was speeding. He'd also been drinking. Our father kept him out of prison, instead working out a deal to send him to rehab. Even though he was released from treatment six months ago, I haven't seen him.

It's better for everyone if we keep it that way.

He swore to me that she'd be safe with him that night and she wasn't. I should have known that he was messed up. I should have driven her to dinner like I'd promised.

Instead, I let her leave with Saint, and he nearly killed her and himself. I'm not sure I'll ever be ready to forgive him—or myself. The nightmares of pulling them from the burning wreckage still wake me in a cold sweat most nights. Guilt rides me hard. Going home won't make it better.

Savannah has been through enough without having to deal with my shit too. Seeing how messed up I am would break her heart into tiny pieces. She deserves a peaceful Christmas with Saint.

"I've got to get moved in and settled," I tell her, my voice gentle. Even though it's the right thing to do, I still hate to do it. "And the School Board has a couple of events planned that I'm required to attend."

"But I miss you," she sighs, breaking my heart.

"I miss you too, brat." I run my hand across the books I just unpacked in my office. Like my house, it's in a state of carefully ordered chaos, with packing boxes stacked in the corners and furniture waiting to be put in place. "What if I come home for your birthday next month? I'll let you drag me out to SB Raceway."

SB Raceway may be her favorite place in San Bernardino. Savannah is competitive as hell, especially when you put her behind the wheel of a go-cart. Saint will just have to keep his distance while I'm in town next month since he's refusing to return to Los Angeles where he lives. If I miss her eighteenth birthday and Christmas, she'll never forgive me. Especially since I already missed Thanksgiving, my birthday, and Mom's birthday.

"Promise?"

"Pinky promise," I swear, smiling. Pinky promises are sacrosanct to my sister. Once made, they're an unbreakable bond she will hold you to no matter what.

"Okay." She falls silent for a moment. "You know you have to forgive him eventually, right?"

"Savannah," I warn her, not willing to discuss the subject with her.

"It was an accident and I'm fine now."

"You nearly died," I growl, pissed off just remembering how close it came. It took two surgeries and weeks in the hospital to save her life. It took months for all the broken bones to heal. And Saint wasn't there for any of it. He was tucked away in a private rehab facility, kicking an addiction he swore he had under control.

"I know that," Savannah huffs at me. "So does he, Sawyer. He's changed so much because of what happened. I wish you would give him a chance to prove it."

I snort, unconvinced.

Saint has always been reckless and wild, with no real direction or plans for his life beyond chasing his next big hit. Savannah's accident is just the latest in a long line of bad behavior from him. We've kept most of it from her because she's so young. She idolizes Saint. If she knew half the shit he's done, it would break her heart.

"You're so stubborn!" she complains, which makes me smile. She's the most tenacious person I've ever met. When she wants something, she won't quit until she gets it. With her big doe eyes and hopeful expression, telling her no is next to impossible. Thank God she uses her powers for good or the world would be in serious trouble.

"Did you get my present?" I ask, changing the subject before she gets all riled up.

"Yes, but Mom won't let me open it until Christmas morning," she says, pouting again. "What is it? The box is huge!"

"It's a surprise." She hates secrets, which means I surprise her as often as possible just to see her squirm. She drives herself crazy trying to figure out what it is.

"You're no fun."

"I'm old," I remind her. "I'm not supposed to be fun."

"You're thirty-six." I can practically hear her eyes roll. "You only act like you're ninety."

I open my mouth to respond and then snap it closed when I hear a woman's voice outside my office.

"Oh, son of a nutcracker!" she cries. Even frustrated, her voice is dulcet and silvery, almost melodious.

Something that sounds curiously like a cymbal crashes to the floor, followed by a series of smaller crashes and inventive, Christmas themed curses from the woman.

What in the world is going on?

"I've gotta go, Savannah." I head toward the door to find out who the woman is and why it sounds like she's destroying the school.

"Fine, but you better not be spending Christmas alone or I'm going to be mad at you."

"Scout's Honor," I lie, crossing my fingers. My sister doesn't need to know that my only plans for Christmas involve a cold beer and the football game on TV. I'll never hear the end of it. And truthfully, it will be lonely enough without her being sad about it too. I've always been home for Christmas, surrounded by our family and friends. Spending the holiday alone isn't any more appealing to me than it is to her.

The clatter outside my office grows louder.

Jesus. What is she carrying out there? An entire drum set?

"Love you, Sawyer," Savannah says.

"Love you too, brat. Behave."

"Never!" She laughs and hangs up on me.

I shove my phone in my pocket and pull the door open, stepping out into the hall.

"Jesus Christ," I mutter, staring in shock at the mess of musical instruments scattered around the hall. And then I gape at the tiny blonde—*elf?*—standing in the middle of the mess, trying to juggle a box that's damn near bigger than she is. One side of it is destroyed, allowing equipment to spill out.

The little elf stares in dismay at the mess surrounding her, seemingly oblivious to my presence. Which is a good thing because I can't seem to take my eyes off her. She's devastatingly beautiful, even dressed in a green and red elf dress with accessories to match.

Wild blonde curls peek from beneath the jaunty hat sitting askew on her head. Her eyes are the darkest forest green I've ever seen. Pink tints her cheeks and her Cupid's Bow lips. Even though she's frowning, I can see the little dimples in her cheeks. She's maybe five-three, with curves sweet enough to make my teeth ache. Her elf dress ends a little above midthigh, with red and white stockings covering her thick thighs and calves.

How she manages to make an elf costume sexy, I don't know, but she pulls it off with frightful ease. My dick stirs, stiffening as I gape at her.

A maraca falls out of the box, landing on one small foot encased in a knee-length boot. The pointy toes make them look like elf shoes.

"Jack Frost!" she shouts, almost dropping the box.

A surprised bark of laughter leaves my lips.

She squeaks, spinning to face me. The box in her arms wobbles dangerously. The bottom is a few strands of meager tape from collapsing into nothing. The rest of it isn't far behind. The box is probably older than she is, and she's maybe twenty-two or twenty-three.

I stride forward to grab it before she manages to upend the rest of her equipment on the floor. I'm not a musician, but my parents bought enough equipment for Saint over the years for me to know it doesn't come cheap.

"I have mace," she blurts out when I stop in front of her.

"Good to know, little elf," I murmur, fighting not to laugh. Call me crazy, but I don't think she'd be happy to know the threat of being pepper-sprayed by a pint-sized woman dressed as an elf isn't particularly intimidating to a guy my size. How she'd even reach her mace with the box in her arms, I don't know. "Maybe wait to use it on me until after we take care of your equipment, hmm?"

Her cheeks turn pink, her gaze bouncing from my face to my outstretched arms. For a minute, I think she's going to refuse to hand over the box, but she quickly changes her mind when another maraca tumbles out, landing between us with a clatter.

"I'm sorry, that was rude," she says, her dulcet voice full of regret as she passes the box to me. "I wasn't expecting anyone to be here. It's late."

"You're here," I point out, amused by the quiet accusation that turns her statement into a question.

"I live here."

"You live in an elementary school?" I hold the box close to my chest to prevent anything else from falling out of it. It's somehow still full of equipment, which shouldn't be possible considering how much of it is on the floor. Good grief, how the hell did she manage to carry it this far? The nearest entrance is a good fifty yards away, and she's little bitty.

"No." Her curls bob as she shakes her head. The tint to her cheeks deepens. She's flustered, which shouldn't be nearly as attractive as it is, but it is. Flustered looks good on her. "Of course I don't live here. I live in a house. I meant to say I *work* here." Her eyes meet mine again, full of curiosity. "Why are you here?"

"I work here too."

"No, you don't. I know everyone who works here."

"How nice," I murmur politely, unable to resist teasing her. She's cute as hell, dancing around asking who the hell I am and why I'm here two days before Christmas. "Should I take this to the music room, or would you like it somewhere else?"

"You know where the music room is located?" She plants her hands on her generous hips, looking at me with patent disbelief.

There she goes, being fucking cute again. Her sass is doing a number on my cock. Which is new. My cock hasn't noticed anyone in years, especially not a staff member and subordinate. Jesus and St. Nick will just have to forgive me for this one though, because this little elf is all too appealing.

If Christmas morning were a person, it would be her. There's a wide-eyed innocence and warmth about her that makes me want to keep her close. Everything seems lighter with her standing in front of me, as if she really is a magical little elf. She even smells like Christmas morning and happy memories.

I bet the kids here love her.

"I do," I say, my lips twitching.

Finally, she gives up waiting for me to volunteer my identity and asks the question she's been dying to ask for the last three minutes.

"Who are you? And please don't say you're robbing the place because I really need help cleaning all this up," she says, flinging her arms out to indicate the mess she's made of the hallway.

"You did a good job of it," I agree. "How did you manage to make it this far with all of this?"

"I'm very coordinated." She scowls at the box. "At least I was until my box decided to betray me."

"I think your box should have been retired two decades ago, little elf."

"It was the only one I could find."

"Sawyer Greenway."

"What?"

"You asked who I am. My name is Sawyer Greenway."

Her eyes go comically wide and her face pales. "*You're* Sawyer Greenway?"

"I am."

"As in our new principal Sawyer Greenway?"

Christ, I'm definitely going to hell because her opened mouth is giving me filthy thoughts about filling it.

"Guilty as charged, little elf."

"Oh fudge," she whispers like Charlie in *A Christmas Story*.

Right then and there, without me even knowing her name, she steals a piece of my heart and claims it as her own.

CHAPTER TWO

LANA

I stare in dismay at my ridiculously hot new boss. Sawyer Greenway is nothing like our former principal, Richard Johnson. He was a short, balding dictator on a personal crusade to suck all the joy out of this place. Sawyer Greenway is a six foot five—at least—monster of a man, with the most beautiful, saddest brown eyes I've ever seen. Although he's clearly American, his flawless olive skin and wicked sharp jawline give him a distinctly Mediterranean appearance. His blue Henley stretches over his broad shoulders and clings to the muscles in his chest. His jeans hug his thighs and firm ass.

His deep laugh rolls over me like thunder in the distance. It's oddly inviting, making me want to laugh with him. Except his laugh is rusty, as if he doesn't use it often. And I'm pretty sure I swallowed my tongue when he said his name.

I threatened to mace my new boss. Awesome.

"What's your name, little elf?" he asks, still laughing at me. Unlike with Mr. Johnson, however, there's no malice in his voice and no judgement in his gaze. He isn't scowling at me either. His full lips are lifted into a half-smile that does strange things to my insides.

I briefly consider giving him a fake name and then moving to somewhere like Bolivia. But my adopted aunt, Leslie Holland, is on the school board here, so disappearing into the great beyond probably wouldn't work out. Besides, I like California. And I love Commodore.

"Lana Winters," I mumble, giving in to the inevitable. "I teach music here."

"So I gathered," he says, flashing that smile at me. Good lord! He has to be close to forty, but when he smiles, he looks like a little boy who is up to no good. It's wickedly hot. "I would shake your hand, but..." He hefts the box in his arms, silently pointing out that his hands are full.

"Jack Frost!" I curse. I forgot all about the ruined box and borrowed equipment all over the floor. He probably thinks I'm a total loon. "I'm so sorry. Um, the music room is this way." I bend to scoop up an armload of equipment and then hurry down the hall.

I think I hear him groan a curse—the box isn't *that* heavy—and then his footsteps sound behind me.

I suck in a deep breath, silently telling myself to get it together. Crushing on the new principal is a bad idea, and I've embarrassed myself enough already. Which is mostly his fault because I didn't expect anyone to be here.

Why *is* he here right now?

"Why are you working so late, Mr. Greenway?" I ask, too curious to keep the question to myself. It's two days until Christmas. No one works this late on Christmas break unless they don't have a choice. Heck, I'm only here to drop off the equipment that the nursing home borrowed for the Christmas pageant.

They can't afford to buy musical equipment. Since I volunteer there and work here, I borrowed some of the school's. Superintendent Thorne said it was okay. Maybe I should tell Mr. Greenway that before he thinks I'm sneaking around?

"I'm not your boss until January. Call me Sawyer. And I'm unpacking my office," he says when we reach the music room.

"On Christmas break?" I spin around to face him, surprised. "Why aren't you with your family?"

He flinches and his half-smile falls into a frown. Pain flashes in his deep brown eyes, sending a bolt of regret spiraling through me.

"I'm sorry," I quickly whisper. "That's none of my business. Ignore me."

"It's fine," he lies. His reassuring smile doesn't meet his eyes, but it makes my heart jump like it's attached to marionette strings. "My parents and siblings are in San Bernardino."

"Oh. That's not too far."

"It's far enough," he murmurs.

Interesting. He wants to be there; I can hear it in his voice. Instead, he's here.

"Do you have any family here?"

He shakes his head.

I gasp. "You're spending Christmas *alone*?"

"You make it sound like a terrible thing." He arches a brow at me, but I don't think he's annoyed with me. He doesn't seem annoyed. Just...sad, and maybe a little amused too.

"I'm sorry. I didn't mean it like that. It's just that being alone on Christmas is so sad." As soon as the explanation leaves my lips, I grimace. I'm not making this any better. For some reason, I keep talking though. "It's a day for being with the ones you love, making memories, and sharing laughter."

"Big Christmas fan, huh?" he teases, following me into the music room.

I flip on the lights and he deposits the box on a table full of instruments the kids use. His gaze sweeps around the room, his eyes growing big as he takes in all the Christmas decorations. Giant snowflakes, brightly colored tinsel, and garland hang everywhere. It looks like Christmas exploded in here, but the kids love it. To be honest, so do I.

Christmas is my favorite time of year. People are much kinder to one another and more generous. Everyone tries to get along with their families and make memories. Growing up, my mom and I didn't have a whole lot, but she scrimped and saved every year to make Christmas magical for me.

We spent hours in the kitchen, baking goodies to take to the nursing home where I still volunteer and to the hospital where mom worked. Aunt Leslie would even come over and help. It was always so much fun to me.

Now that I'm older, we still keep to the same traditions.

"I love Christmas," I murmur, smiling at the memories.

"Me too," he says, his voice soft. "It's my baby sister's favorite day of the year." The sadness is back in his eyes again, turning them from deep brown to pure midnight. I don't know what happened to divide his family and prevent him from going home, but it makes my heart hurt for him. He seems like a genuinely good man who truly misses his siblings and parents. He shouldn't have to spend his first Christmas in a new city alone.

"You're spending Christmas with me," I say before I lose the nerve. Inviting the ridiculously hot, single principal to spend Christmas with you probably isn't strictly professional, but my mom and Aunt Leslie will understand. If they were here, they would do the same thing.

He blinks long lashes at me. "You want to spend Christmas with me?"

"Yes."

"Why?"

Because the thought of you spending it alone is breaking my heart.

"Why not?" I retort, and then grab a rolling cart before he can ask me anything else. "We should get the hall cleaned up."

Crap. Maybe I should let him out of helping me? I consider it for a moment, remember how much equipment is out there, and quickly decide against letting him off the hook. Some of it is heavy. And I like talking to him.

There's something about him that's so...calming? Maybe that's not the right word. Or maybe I'm crazy. I don't know. But being near him is peaceful and soothing. Maybe it's the way he smells like the forest and the ocean all tangled up together. I'm not sure. But something about him feels...right. It makes me want to stay near him.

He's quiet as we head back down the hall. The squeaky wheel on the cart is the only sound between us. The silence is comfortable though, easy.

"How long have you been a principal?" I ask as we round the corner, leaving behind the colorful artwork hanging on bulletin boards all up and down the hall. This one is less colorful, duller and institutional-like. Principal Johnson hated having artwork hanging outside the administration offices.

"This is my first rodeo."

"Really?" I turn my head to look at Sawyer, surprised.

He nods, giving me another of those half-smiles. "I was the assistant dean at a small private college before accepting this position. Hopefully, I'm not rubbish at it."

"Why did you leave?"

"I needed a change of pace," he says, glancing away. That look is back in his eyes, the one that squeezes my heart into a vise and makes me want to hug him.

"Can I give you a word of advice?"

"Of course."

"The teachers here are incredible. Everyone loves these kids and will fight hard for them. But if they aren't receptive to you right out of the gate, it's not you. Um, our last principal was..."

"A dick?" he supplies when I flounder.

"Yes!" I'm so glad he said it, so I didn't have to be the one to do it. "Johnson terrorized the school and made everyone miserable. The kids were scared of him. The teachers avoided him. It wasn't pleasant."

"I've heard," he says, drawing to a stop when we reach the first of the scattered instruments. He reaches down to scoop up a tambourine and a maraca. "Thorne filled me in on the situation. It's been rough going around here for a while, from what I understand."

"Johnson made this place feel more like a prison than a school."

"Why did you stay?" He catches my gaze as he drops the instruments on the cart, genuine curiosity crinkling the corners of his eyes and furrowing his brow. It's not a passing curiosity either, not something small. It's almost as if he needs to know on some level I'm not even sure I understand.

"Because of the kids. I love them so much. I didn't want to abandon them or let them down. We all did what we could to protect them and blunt his impact. I guess we all stayed because we were worried about who would take our places if we left," I admit with a self-conscious shrug, bending to grab one of the cymbals and a set of drumsticks. "Most of us live in this community. These kids are our neighbors, our families. You don't abandon family."

"Do you have kids, little elf?" he asks, his eyes locked on my face as I set the items in the cart.

"No," I whisper, caught up in his gaze. His eyes are so damn beautiful. If they are the doorways to our souls like everyone says they are, then I'm pretty sure his soul is powerfully bright. I could get lose in his eyes and the warmth shining there.

"Do you want kids?"

"So bad."

He reaches out, moving slow as if to give me time to step away and shut him down. I don't. I'm not sure I could even if I wanted to do it. My body is frozen, locked in place as we stare at one another, something vast and powerful growing between us.

His hand touches my cheek, his knuckles gliding down the side of it.

My entire body hums like thousands of Christmas lights flickering to life.

I think he feels it too because he sucks in a sharp breath. Heat darkens his expression, turning him fierce. He takes a step closer to me. Or maybe I move closer to him. I'm not sure, but somehow, we end up standing so close together I can feel the heat coming off his body.

"Do you really want to spend Christmas with me?" he asks, his voice velvety soft. He touches one of my curls, gently tucking it behind my ear.

"Yes," I whisper.

"Why?"

"I don't like the way it feels to think of you spending the holiday alone." I'm unable to contain the words when he's staring at me like they're important to him. "It...hurts."

His long lashes flutter. He leans forward and brushes his lips across my cheek.

I don't know why I do it, but I turn my head toward him. Our lips slide together in a sweet kiss that sears me all the way to my soul. He makes a sound that's halfway between a groan and a growl. His tongue touches my bottom lip as if he's tasting me and then he pulls back.

"Thank you," he says, but I'm not sure if he's thanking me for my honesty, if he's thanking me for caring, if his gratitude is for the kiss, or for the invitation. Perhaps it's a combination of all four. All I know for sure is that the shadows in his eyes are lighter and the smile that curves his lips is genuine.

For now, that's enough.

CHAPTER THREE

SAWYER

"I come bearing gifts," Lana says, holding up two giant grocery bags when I throw open the front door bright and early the next morning. Her cheeks are pink from the wind and her hair is tousled. The weak winter sun lights up the blonde strands, making her look as if she has a golden halo dancing around her head.

I scrub a hand down my face, blinking. Christ, she looks edible.

"Oh no," she whispers, her face falling as she takes in my sweats, t-shirt, and wild hair. "I thought we said eight. Did I wake you up?"

"No, I've been up." In more ways than one. My cock hasn't taken a rest since I met her yesterday. I've jerked the fucker raw and he's still stirring in my pants. But I don't think she wants to hear that I spent half the night getting off to filthy fantasies of her.

I couldn't help it.

Even in my sleep, I smelled her intoxicating blend of fresh pine and sweet holly blossoms. She's crawled under my skin and taken up residence there. For the first time in months, I feel at ease, peaceful. As if the weight on my shoulders has been lessened. For once, my dreams weren't full of memories of pulling Savannah's broken body from the mangled wreckage of Saint's car. I dreamed of a cheery little elf with bright eyes, pink cheeks, and the sweetest laugh I've ever heard.

The wind howls outside, making her shiver.

"Shit." I hold the door open wide for her to come inside. It's not particularly cold out, but there's a definite bite in the wind blowing in from the Bay. I think it's going to storm. "Come in, little star."

"Little star?" Her eyes light up, a smile on her face. Those dimples of hers make me want to toss her over my shoulder and carry her to my bed. "I thought you were going to insist on sticking with the elf thing."

"I'm trying something new," I murmur, gritting my teeth when she slips by me, passing so close her scent swirls around me and my dick stands straight up again. What I really want to call her is *mine*, but I'm not sure she's ready to hear that yet.

"Your house is incredible, Sawyer," she says, looking around with wide eyes at the place. The newly renovated Gothic is gorgeous inside and out. The original floors and decorative molding lend a certain understated elegance to the place, making it seem like the type of home where you'd raise a family rather than a last-minute acquisition. "How did you find this place on such short notice?"

"My father is in real estate," I murmur, shoving the door closed to keep the wind from whipping through. "He has connections all over the state. This place was coming up on the market when I took the job, so I jumped on it."

"I'm jealous." She pouts at me, her bottom lip poking out. I want to bite it. "I live in a shoebox crammed in between two other shoeboxes, in a row of shoeboxes."

Is it too soon to convince her to move in with me?

Shit. Probably so.

"You said you came bearing gifts," I say, nodding at the bags in her hands. "Am I allowed to carry them for you?"

"Yes, please." She holds them out to me with a sweet smile. "Where's your kitchen?"

"That way." I point her in the right direction and then grin when she immediately sets off to find it. She doesn't wait around for permission or for me to take the lead. She just strikes off on her own adventure. I love it. I follow behind her, watching the way her wide hips sway back and forth.

"You're still unpacking?" she says, glancing at me over her shoulder as we pass through the maze of boxes in the living room.

"Unfortunately."

"I'll help."

"You want to help me unpack?"

"Sure. Why not? It'll keep us busy while everything is baking."

I can think of more interesting ways to keep us busy.

"What are we baking?"

"Cookies." She flashes me a bright, happy smile that leaves me weak in the knees. "Lots and lots of cookies. I brought most everything we need, but please tell me you have a stand mixer."

"I do." My mom insisted I needed one two years ago. The only time it's ever been used was when she and Savannah used it. I can cook, but I leave baking to the professionals.

"Is it unpacked?"

"The kitchen is mostly done."

"Oh, thank God," she breathes. "Mixing cookie dough is a full body workout." Her gaze dances up and down my body. "You probably do those every day."

"More or less," I murmur, fighting a smile at her tone.

"I hate working out." She scowls like the thought makes her want to set the gym on fire. "My mom and I usually go at least two days a week though."

We pass through the dining room into the kitchen.

"Father Christmas, this room is amazing!" Lana says, stopping to survey the space.

"Father Christmas?" I chuckle at her enthusiasm and set the bags down on the island. The kitchen is one of my favorite rooms in the house. It's massive and bright, with natural light filtering in from windows all over the room. It reminds me of being home.

My mom is always in the kitchen, cooking and baking or simply nursing a cup of coffee at the table. Dad had her kitchen renovated a few years ago to give her more space to work with. Getting her out of there is next to impossible now. She would live in there if he'd let her.

"I'm cleaning up my vocabulary."

"By replacing swear words with Christmas words?"

Lana turns her nose up at my teasing, which is just fucking adorable. And then she narrows her eyes on me. "Just wait until you drop your first curse word in front of a room full of eight-year-olds. See who's laughing then."

"Probably the eight-year-olds," I tease.

She glances down and then quickly jerks her eyes back up toward mine. Her cheeks turn from pink to red and her eyes get glassy. "You should go put some clothes on while I get everything ready," she says, her voice strangled.

"I am dressed."

"Um, I can see your...staff," she whisper-hisses like she's trying to keep it a secret.

I hesitate for a moment, torn between doing the right thing and being a gentleman and doing what I really want to do and kissing the shit out of her. I settled for option three. "He's been this way since you kissed me last night."

She gulps, but she doesn't look like she wants to slap me. I take that as a good sign.

"I've been thinking about that kiss non-fucking-stop."

"M-me too," she whispers, her voice shaky.

"I'm going to kiss you today. Potentially often. You okay with that?"

"You're my boss. Won't that cause...problems for you?"

"I'm not your boss yet," I remind her. Even if I were, I doubt Sebastian Thorne would have much to say about it considering that his wife is one of our teachers. "If you want to keep things strictly professional, I'll try."

"But that's not what you want," she says.

"It's not." I hold her gaze, so she knows I'm not messing around here. "I'm dying to make you mine. But if that's not what you want, I'll back off." I grimace. "I'll *try* to back off."

She swallows hard. "I don't want you to back off," she whispers, staring at me from beneath her lashes. "I feel...drawn to you for some reason. Does that sound silly?"

"There's nothing silly about you, Lana." I stride toward her and slide my hand into her hair to tip her head back. Her wide eyes meet mine. Before she can think about it too much, I lean down and kiss her hard on the mouth and then back away. "I'll go get dressed."

By the time I make it back to the kitchen, Lana's managed to turn it into a bakery. Christmas music drifts from her phone. The countertops are covered with an explosion of bowls, baking sheets, cookie cutters, and enough ingredients to feed an army.

I don't think she was exaggerating when she said we were making lots and lots of cookies. She looks happy as a clam surrounded by all her tools.

I stand in the doorway, watching her as she dances around my kitchen, singing her heart out and shimmying her hips. She's captivating, so incredibly beautiful she takes my breath away. Her dulcet voice is absolutely stunning. She should be singing in front of crowds.

For some reason I can't explain, I already know she would hate that type of life.

She's too pure. A life on the road would drain her dry and leave her feeling empty. She needs love and affection and children and home. That's her happy place, the place where she thrives. Anything less would stifle her. She really is a magical little elf, a bright star, shining like a beacon to guide weary souls home.

"I'm marrying your kitchen," she says, flashing those dimples when she sees me watching her. She doesn't get flustered or embarrassed at having been caught dancing. She doesn't even really stop. She just sends teasing laughter my way and keeps on arranging everything to her liking.

I prowl toward her across the room, unable to keep from smiling back at her. It feels like it's been years since I've smiled as often as I have since I met her. When she's near, the guilt lies quietly instead of constantly plaguing me. It's a good feeling.

"You can't marry my kitchen, little star," I murmur, circling around the island toward her. She's going to marry me.

"Can so."

"No."

"You're no fun. Where are your food sprinkles?"

"Food sprinkles?"

"Spices. The stuff you put on food to make it taste like magic?" she sasses, hands on her hips and a smirk on her lips. "I forgot cinnamon."

Christ. I think I love her.

I rake my gaze down her body, smiling wider when I see that she's kicked her shoes off somewhere and is wearing mismatched Christmas socks. "I don't think you can reach them."

She gasps in mock outrage. "Are you calling me short, Mr. Greenway?"

"If the shoe fits." I crowd close to her and reach over her head to open the cabinet where all my spices are kept. I don't even know what half of them are used for, but my mom and Savannah have a tendency of bringing me things they think I need even when I really don't. I guess they think being a bachelor makes me helpless. Letting them fuss over me and fill my house with shit I don't need nor use makes them happy, so I let them get away with it.

"You smell good," Lana says. Her body presses closer to mine as if she's trying to smell me and then a little purring sound comes from her. Her hand skims along my stomach.

My dick instantly reacts, pointing like a divining rod at her.

"You're killing me here," I groan, grabbing the cinnamon.

"Sorry," she says even as her soft laugh says different. She removes her hand. "Did you put on cologne?"

"No. I showered." I drop the bottle of cinnamon into her outstretched hand and close the cabinet before doing a little smelling of my own. "You smell like Christmas."

Her dimples appear again.

Fuck it.

I swoop, caging her in against the island. As soon as she tips her head back to look at me, I press my lips to hers, kissing her like I've been dying to do since she first kissed me last night. Only this isn't a sweet little peck. I boost her up onto the counter with my hand around her waist. Pans hit the floor with a clatter, but I don't care.

I lick into her mouth. Her taste hits my system hard, annihilating my self-control. Jesus, she even *tastes* like Christmas, all sugar and spice and everything nice.

She kisses me back just as desperately, her hands clutched in my hair. Our tongues dance together and then apart as little whimpers and moans whisper from her. She's purring like a happy little kitten again.

Kissing her is a revelation. She's unschooled, eager, and so damn sweet. The combination is intoxicating as hell. She learns quickly, mimicking me as I pour my desire for her into our kiss. When we're both gasping for breath and she's trembling in my arms, I back off, placing a softer kiss to her lips before I rest my forehead against hers.

"Wow," she whispers. "Can we do that again?"

A burst of laughter escapes my lips. "You're something else, you know that?"

"Is that a good thing or a bad thing?"

"It's a good thing." I kiss her again to reassure her. "It's a really damn good thing."

"Okay then."

CHAPTER FOUR

LANA

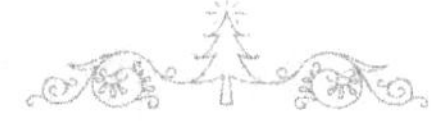

"I'm not keeping you from your family today, am I?" Sawyer asks, eyeing me across the island as he pipes icing onto his sugar cookies. I think they're supposed to be angels, but they look more like those little throwing stars ninjas use. He's terrible at baking. Which is adorable to me.

Spending the morning with him has been so much fun. Even though he's a little quiet, he's wickedly clever and so sweet. He teases me just to rile me up, grinning the whole time. I like it because he seems so sad sometimes, like there's a heavy weight on his shoulders.

He keeps stealing kisses, but I don't mind. I *really* like those. I haven't kissed many people before. Dating just wasn't ever a big priority for me. The few times I have gone out, I didn't have fun like I'm having with Sawyer. I couldn't wait to leave. The thought of leaving here makes my stomach hurt.

"It's just me and my mom," I say, turning to pop another pan of chocolate chip cookies into the oven. I brush my hair back with my arm to keep from getting flour in it. "She's a trauma nurse. She had to work today so she can be off tomorrow."

"What do you normally do on Christmas Eve?"

"Bake cookies to deliver to the nursing home and hospital. And then we watch Christmas chick flicks." I smile at him. "But don't worry, I won't make you watch them with me."

"I'll have you know," he says, smirking at me, "I'm an expert in Christmas chick flicks. The Hallmark Channel is my jam."

"Your jam?" I throw my head back and laugh. "Name one Hallmark movie."

He sets his icing bag down and carefully wipes his hands on a hand towel, his brows furrowed as if he's thinking hard about his answer. And then he lifts those gorgeous deep brown eyes to me and gives me that little boy smile. "I don't have a fucking clue," he admits cheerfully. "But I'm going to go with something about a small-town girl down on her luck."

I shake my head at him, unable to keep from smiling like a crazy person.

"In all seriousness," he says, picking up his icing bag again. "I've been watching them with my little sister for years. Christmas is her favorite season. She eats, breathes, and sleeps the holiday from October until January."

"How old is she?"

"She'll be eighteen next month."

"She's a lot younger than you."

"She's adopted."

"Really?"

He nods. "My mom had some complications when my brother, Saint, was born. She wasn't able to have more kids, so they adopted Savannah. Her parents were good friends with my parents. They were killed in a car wreck when she was a baby."

"That's really sad," I murmur, "but really sweet of your parents to bring her home so she would always be with people who loved her parents. I bet she adores you and your brother."

"Yeah, she does." He smiles, but it doesn't touch his eyes this time.

"Can I ask a question that's none of my business?"

"You want to know why I'm not at home," he guesses.

"It's obvious how much your family means to you."

"They do," he says, and then carefully ices the cookie in front of him. Just when I'm about to open my mouth to apologize for being nosy, he looks up at me again. "Every year on Thanksgiving, we have a big family dinner. My mom wasn't feeling well last year, so instead of her trying to cook dinner the night before and then again on Thanksgiving, we decided that we'd all go out to eat." He swallows hard. "Savannah was supposed to ride with me, but Saint had just gotten a new car and he wanted to show it off. I had an errand to run, so I agreed to let her ride with him." His hands shake so he sets the icing bag down and grips onto the edge of the counter.

He looks a little lost, so I circle the island and push my way into his personal space to wrap my arms around him. His muscles are rigid with tension, but after a second, he hugs me back. I lay my head against his chest, listening to the way his heart pounds. It seems so loud and strong for a heart that's as broken as I sense his is.

"I was a mile from the restaurant when I heard the crash," he rasps. "Instantly, I just knew it was them. I felt it in my gut so I just...floored it to get there. I was the first one to arrive at the scene. Saint had taken a curve too fast and lost control. The car flipped over an embankment and caught fire." His entire body trembles so I hold him tighter, trying to be strong enough to hold him together. "They were trapped in the vehicle. I still have nightmares about pulling them out of the wreckage before the flames got to them."

"Oh, Sawyer. I am so sorry," I whisper, tears filling my eyes at what he must have gone through trying to save the siblings he loves so much.

"Saint had cuts and bruises, but Savannah...Savannah was in bad shape," he murmurs, his voice a gritty rasp that breaks my heart to hear it. "They had to airlift her out of there to the hospital. Her first surgery was a couple of hours later. Her second was the next day. She spent months recovering. Even now, all the bones she broke still cause her problems."

"You blame yourself."

He nods his head against mine, his breath a painful shudder. "They found a bottle of whiskey at the scene. Saint had been drinking. I knew that he'd been drinking more than usual since his last tour ended, but he swore to me that he hadn't touched a bottle that day. I'm not even sure if I really believed him or if I let her get in the car with him because I was impatient to run my errand."

"It's not your fault, Sawyer," I whisper, tilting my head back to look at him. My heart hurts at the bleak look in his eyes, as if his soul is bleeding and raw. The sight of his pain sends tears trickling down my cheeks. "You never would have let her get in that car if you'd known. You wouldn't have let him get in that car either."

"I should have known." He wipes my tears with shaking hands. "Saint is the wild child in our family. It's only gotten progressively worse since his band was signed when he turned twenty-one. He's reckless and irresponsible and does things just because he can. It's always been my job to watch out for him and Savannah, to make sure he doesn't get too far out of hand."

"Wait. Are you talking about Saint Green from *Vengeful Saints*?"

"My brother," he says, his voice flat.

"Wow. I had no idea." *Vengeful Saints* is one of the most successful rock bands around. Saint Green—Saint Greenway, I guess—is the bad boy of the group, the lead singer. He's always in the tabloids. At least he was...until he was involved in a car accident last year. His little sister was critically injured. "You guys seem so different."

Sawyer gives me a grim look. "Like I said, he's reckless and irresponsible. Savannah idolizes him though. They've always been thick as thieves. She's missed him terribly."

"You stayed away so she could spend the holiday with him," I whisper.

He shrugs like it's not a big deal but we both know it is. "Saint and I haven't seen each other since the day of the accident," he murmurs. "We both said things we can't take back. But he's home for Christmas this year, so it's better for everyone if I'm not."

I don't think that's true. He and Saint may be at odds, but I'm guessing his family misses him just as much as they missed Saint while he was gone. From what I remember, Saint checked himself into rehab and disappeared from the public eye for six months. When he reappeared, he was...different. He stopped appearing in tabloids, stopped doing a lot of things.

I don't think Sawyer is the only one who blames himself for what happened to Savannah. I don't think he's the only one still hurting. I also don't think Sawyer is ready to hear that right now.

The rift between him and Saint is something they have to mend on their own. I can't force him to do it. I can't even make him go home for Christmas. But I *can* show him that he isn't the awful person he thinks he is.

He might doubt himself, but I don't. I've known him for all of a day, and I know beyond a shadow of a doubt that he never, ever would have let either of them get into that car if he'd even suspected that Saint had been drinking.

He may be upset with his brother, but he loves him as deeply as he loves their little sister. He says he stayed away so Savannah can see Saint. I think he stayed away to give Saint the same time with her. That's the kind of selfless, loving person he is. Even though he's hurting and lonely, he put them first the best way he knew how. I don't think he realizes that keeping himself from them is only going to hurt everyone more. It's only going to hurt *him* more.

I'm going to find a way to help him see the man I see when I look at him. And I see so much in him. He's the selfless, loving brother who would do anything for his siblings, and the gentle giant who upended his whole life to help protect a school full of kids he's never met. He's the gentlemanly stranger willing to drop everything to help me clean up my own mess...and the sweet, lonely man who let me invade his home and his life without a single complaint.

I know a thing or two about men who don't believe they're worthy of love, and this one is so incredibly worthy. I'm going to find a way to heal his heart and make him see what I see. If he can't fight for himself right now, I'll fight for him. Even if I have to fight him.

"How big is your fridge?" I ask, reaching up to touch his jaw.

He blinks at me, confused.

"Will it hold all these cookies?"

He glances at the bowls still filled with cookie dough and then nods. "It'll hold them," he says, his eyes scanning across my face. "Why?"

"Because there's someone I want you to meet."

CHAPTER FIVE

SAWYER

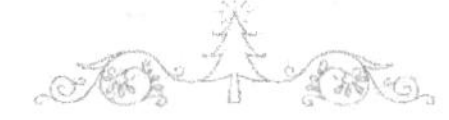

"What are you up to, little elf?" I ask Lana, eyeing her sideway as I navigate through the gates of a cemetery in the Tenderloin district of the city. She's perched in the passenger seat of my truck, commanding me like a tiny queen.

"You'll see," she says, her dulcet voice not giving anything away. "Oh! Turn right! Turn right!"

I curse and make a sharp right onto the gravel drive leading deeper into the worn-down cemetery. The grass is patchy and faded flowers hang limply in baskets and arrangements on tombstones. Some of the tombstones are so old they're covered in moss.

The truck bounces over a series of deep, muddy potholes in the gravel lane, sending us both sliding back and forth until our seatbelts lock.

"Sorry." Lana looks at me with big eyes once the truck levels out on the other side of the potholes. "I should have warned you. Every time it rains, the gravel washes out."

"It's all good," I murmur. "It'll take a hell of a lot more than a last-minute turn and a few potholes to take down this truck."

"Turn right at the very last driveway on the right. It's beside the old angel statue. And then park under the giant oak tree," Lana instructs as if she's been here a thousand times. She cocks her head to the side and then smiles. "Oh, I love this song."

I reach to turn it up, but her horrified squeak stops me mid-motion.

"You can't play loud music in a cemetery," she says, making it sound as if I intended to set up a stage and throw a party. The look of horror on her face makes me want to kiss her again.

"I don't think they'll mind," I murmur, but I don't turn it up any louder.

"They might."

Her haughty sniff pulls a chuckle from my lips. I shake my head at her. My little elf marches to the beat of her own drum, but she's still a rule-follower. If she gets any cuter, we'll be giving the souls at rest here more of a show than I'm strictly comfortable with.

Lana tilts her head back. Her beautiful voice rings out around us as she sings along to the radio, belting out the lyrics to *What Child is This?* as if she were born to sing. Her voice is clear and strong, and incredibly powerful for such a little bitty thing. I listen in awe, goosebumps rising on my arms.

She notices and smiles. "I love singing."

And I love how comfortable she is with herself, how confident she is. She throws her whole heart into everything she does and never apologizes for it. Whether she's singing, dancing, or taking over my kitchen, she never hesitates. When she's happy, she's joyous. When she's sad, I'm pretty sure the angels weep. She shines bright as a star.

There is something so peaceful about being near her, as if this is where I'm meant to be and loving her is what I was born to do. I think it may have been. In a matter of hours, she's managed to wriggle her way into my heart, claiming it as her own. Everything is brighter with her here, better. She makes me want to be better, to *do* better.

She gives me...hope.

"You have a beautiful voice, Lana." I take the last right by a stone angel near the back of the cemetery. It's so old the face has eroded, leaving it expressionless. The giant oak is situated just on the other side. The bare branches shoot upward like bony fingers reaching toward the heavens.

Like the angel, the tree stands in testament to the age of this cemetery.

"Thank you," Lana says, and then hums the last few bars of the song.

"Wait for me," I murmur when she unlatches her seatbelt to climb out of the truck. She's so short I had to lift her into it. I don't want her breaking her leg trying to climb down without help.

"Okay," she agrees, settling back.

I turn off the engine and pop my door open before stepping out. Gravel crunches beneath my feet. The smell of rain is stronger out here. So is the unique scent I've begun to associate with this city—saltwater, brine, and humanity.

I circle around to the passenger side.

"Thank you," Lana says politely, letting me lift her to the ground.

Feeling her curves beneath my hands makes my entire body ache. She's so soft.

She slips her hand into mine. There's a look in her eyes that's new, a steely determination that is as unique to her as the scent of San Francisco is to this city. This little elf is on a mission and won't be stopped until she's completed it. Her grit makes my dick hard.

Then again, everything this magical little elf does puts me in the same state of aching need. I've never wanted anyone the way I want her. Hell, I've never wanted *anything* the way I want her. Talking to her is simple, being with her is effortless.

"So, why are we here?" I ask, standing as close to her as possible to block the wind from her. The horizon to the west has darkened significantly since we left the house. The storm will be here within the next hour or two. I want to have her back home, tucked up safely in my kitchen by then.

"Come with me and I'll show you." She takes off through the grass.

I follow behind, smiling as she practically dances to keep from stepping on any part of the graves we weave between. She even reads the names off the tombstones and whispers apologies when she can't completely avoid stepping on them.

A few rows in, she draws to a stop at the side of a grave. Its flat, grassy top hints at its age. My stomach sinks at the sight of the festive flowers and little snowmen lining the top of the small tombstone. They hint at just how much she loved the man buried here. His name was Sam Austin. He died young.

"This is my dad," she says, her soft statement confirming my suspicion.

"I'm sorry, little star. I didn't know you'd lost your dad." Judging from the date of death, she lost him when she was just a little girl. She couldn't have been more than ten.

"You can't really lose someone you never had, can you?" She slips her hand from mine and kneels to adjust one of the arrangements that's tipped over on his grave. "I never met him."

Shit.

"I'm sorry, sweetheart."

"Me too." She stands up again, reaching for my hand. "He died when I was nine. Before that, he stayed away." She turns her head to look at me, her expression somber. "He did some things when he was younger, things he wasn't proud of doing. He spent the first seven years of my life in prison. He came to see my mom once after he was released, but he was gone before I got home from school."

"Jesus, Lana," I whisper, my heart cracking in half for her. "I'm so damn sorry."

"He didn't believe he deserved me and my mom after what he did," she announces, matter of fact.

"What..." I have to swallow to work moisture back into my mouth. "What did he do?"

"He stole a car. The keys were in the ignition and it was running. He didn't stop to think about why." Her brows furrow, a shadow passing across her beautiful face. "The police found him about an hour later. They chased him for over an hour. He wrecked twice before he finally stopped."

"He stopped?"

She nods. "The baby in the backseat started to cry."

"Jesus Christ," I rasp. "Did...?"

She shakes her head, allowing me to exhale a relieved breath. "Once he realized there was a baby back there, he pulled over and surrendered. No one was harmed, but for two hours, that little baby's parents were terrified they'd never see their daughter again. My mom was pregnant with me when it happened. Seeing their grief when they came to get the baby, knowing that he could have seriously hurt an innocent infant...it messed him up. I guess he stayed away to punish himself."

"I'm so damn sorry, Lana," I murmur, wrapping my arms around her.

"Me too. But the thing is...he didn't just punish himself by clinging to that guilt and banishing himself from my life. Even if he didn't mean to do it, he punished me and my mom too." Her eyes meet mine, bottomless forest green searing into me so fiercely I feel her words resonate in my soul. "I never got to know my dad because he couldn't let it go and be with me and my mom."

I stare at her in silence, not sure what to say to that, not sure there are words to make her feel better or heal the hurt that had to have caused her. If she were mine, I'd never let her go. Every day, I'd fight to be worthy of her, to stay close to her.

"Don't punish your family because you can't forgive yourself, Sawyer," she whispers. "You're a genuine, selfless man and you love them so much. Don't let a mistake destroy who you are inside. You *never* would have let them get into that car had you known. Even if you don't know that, I do. Let it go and forgive yourself before the guilt consumes you like it did my dad."

She makes me *want* to let it go. Staring at her, holding her in my arms, I want to be the man she sees, the one she brought out here because she believed he was worthy of hearing this story and meeting the man she loves so fiercely even though she never met him. I don't think she lets many people know this piece of her history, but she shared it with me.

I want to be worthy of that gift. I want to love her the way she deserves to be loved: not with the jagged pieces of a heart shattered by guilt, but with every fiber of my heart and soul.

And to do that, I have to face what happened. I have to find a way to let it go.

"I would have moved heaven and hell to protect Savannah," I admit, holding Lana as tightly as I dare. Tremors wrack me, shaking loose the secret shame I've tried so hard to hide from everyone, myself included. I drag it out into the light for her, give her the truth I've never shared with anyone. "But I didn't do the same for Saint. I knew he was drowning but I was so fucking *frozen* that I just let it happen. I pretended I didn't see what was going on because it was easier than admitting that my little brother had a problem I couldn't fix for him. It kills me that I wasn't there when he needed me."

"Fixing him wasn't your responsibility, Sawyer. All he needs from you, all he's ever needed from you, is for you to love him," she whispers. Her arms encircle my waist. Her head rests against my chest. She hugs me so fiercely I think maybe she's trying to stitch me back together with the strength of her embrace. But she's been stitching all my broken pieces back together since I met her.

I needed a miracle, and God sent me one in the form of a magical little elf with a soul bright enough to light up even the deepest, darkest corners of my heart. He might not have meant for me to keep her, but she's mine now.

I'm not letting her go.

By the time we make it back to my place, the storm is pounding the coast on its way inland. Rain sheets down around us and gusts of wind rock the truck. I scoop Lana up into my arms and make a mad dash through the down-pour to the front door.

She wraps her arms around my neck and tilts her face up, laughing as the cold rain drenches us both in a matter of seconds. I juggle her in my arms so I can unlock the front door, my heart feeling unburdened in a way it hasn't for a long time. I feel *hope* in a way I haven't in a long time.

I think I needed someone to remind me that it's not my job to fix or save Saint. He has to fix himself. All I can do is love him. I don't know if I can mend our relationship or if I should even try to repair it...but I do know I can't keep punishing myself for being human. He and I may never get back to where we were when we were younger. He may never grow up and learn to take responsibility for himself. But his path is his to walk. I can't do it for him or control where it takes him. All I can do is focus on the things I can control.

"Put me down," Lana demands, kicking her feet once we're over the threshold. Her sweet laughter washes over me, stroking like a thousand caresses across my skin.

The rain is frigid, but the chill doesn't register as my core temperature rises several degrees. Blood heats in my veins and heads south, stiffening my cock. I shove the door closed with my foot and carry her straight up the stairs, not stopping until we're in the master bedroom.

"Put me down, crazy man!" she laughs, wriggling in my hold. And then she looks around and blinks, sobering. "Oh. Wow."

My stuff is still mostly in boxes, but I can't deny how gorgeous this room is. The hardwood floors gleam beneath thick black rugs and cream walls. The back wall is glass, the French doors letting out onto a balcony that overlooks the hills and valleys of the city.

My bed rests against the opposite wall, the ornate wood and black and gold bedding giving the room a decadent, dramatic feel. The rest of the furniture matches. Savannah helped me pick it out before I moved. She did a damn good job because the room looks masculine but still manages to be inviting.

I carry Lana into the en-suite bathroom before setting her on her feet. She spins in a circle, gaping like...well, like a little elf discovering the magic of Christmas for the first time. She's so damn beautiful. She takes my breath away.

"Sawyer, your house is spectacular," she says. "I could seriously live in this bathroom."

"You think so?" I reach in to start the shower before I grab a towel to wrap her in while the water heats. The bathroom is large, with a shower big enough to hold a family and a whirlpool tub that stands in an alcove. His and hers vanities stretch across one wall, and the toilet is separated in its own little area. The marble walls and wood-grain tile appear seamless, like extensions of one another.

"Uh-huh," she whispers and then she cocks her head to the side. "Maybe I should have been a principal instead of a music teacher."

"We don't make that much," I say, chuckling at her. There's no way I could afford this place on my salary alone. Housing in San Francisco is notoriously expensive. "But I've made some good investments that paid off."

"You're a unicorn." She grins at me, water dripping down her face.

"A unicorn?"

"Yep. You're hot, intelligent, modest, single, and financially secure," she explains, ticking them off on her fingers while I wrap the towel around her. "Women probably throw themselves at you."

"Only one woman exists to me."

"Oh yeah?" Another teasing grin dances at her lips and through her eyes.

"Yeah."

"Lucky her," she whispers, her gaze dropping to my lips.

"Lucky me," I murmur, using my hold on the towel to tug her body closer to me. I brush wet strands of her hair back from her face with my free hand, smiling at her. Even soaked with rain, she's the sweetest little thing I've ever seen. "You're all wet, little star."

"Rain does that," she teases, tilting her head back to look at me. The teasing doesn't reflect in her eyes this time. Those are somber and serious, concern burning in their depths. "Are you all right?"

For most people, questions like that are just questions, asked because it's the polite thing to do when confronted with any sort of raw emotion. Lana isn't most people. When she asks, I feel her concern and the compassion that drives it. She truly wants to know how I'm feeling since my confession. We didn't talk much on the drive home.

"Yeah," I promise, tucking another strand of hair behind her ear. "I have a lot of shit to think about, but I think I'm going to be all right."

"Good." She burrows into my arms, cuddling up against my chest. "I want that for you. It can be your Christmas present to me."

"I think that's supposed to be my gift from you," I say, grinning at how damn precious she is. A heart like hers...God, the world needs more of her gentle spirit and unerring love. We would all be better off with more women like her shining their light in the world.

"Nope. Me cleaning up the mess I made in your kitchen is my gift to you," she says with a laugh and then she shivers in my arms.

Shit. She's probably freezing by now.

"Come on. Into the shower to warm up," I demand, swinging her up into my arms to carry her the short distance.

"Sawyer!" she squeaks when she realizes I intend to put her in the shower fully clothed. "You're going to get me all wet!"

"Hate to break it to you, baby, but you're already all wet." I pull her towel off and toss it over the side of the bathtub before stepping into the shower with her.

"Sawyer!" she shouts, sputtering in outrage. Her teeth chatter at the end. Her cheeks and nose are pink from the cold rain too.

"Shh, sweet girl," I soothe, yanking my t-shirt off over my head and tossing it toward the corner of the shower. "Just let me warm you up before you freeze to death."

"I'm not c-cold," she lies, her gaze roving all over my chest.

I'm not a vain man. Looking good has never been a priority in my life and what women think of me has never mattered. I've been too focused on my career to date much. I work out because I enjoy the physical activity after working at a desk all day. But the way Lana is looking at me makes me damn glad I enjoy my time at the gym.

I keep my eyes on her as I kick my boots off and slide them out of the way. The pulse in her throat flutters beneath her alabaster skin as I pop the button on my jeans.

"Ditch the clothes, Lana," I order her, my voice soft. "You need to warm up."

"Oh, I'm definitely warming up," she says, reaching out to place a hand against the wall of the shower. "Jolly Santa, Sawyer. How much time do you spend at the gym to look like that?"

"A lot," I grunt, working my jeans down my legs. It's not easy to do when they're wet and my dick is hard as a rock and she's looking at me like I'm the best thing she's ever seen. I finally manage to get them down and kick them toward the corner. They land against the wall with a wet plop and then slide down.

Lana gulps audibly.

"Clothes, little star," I growl, prowling across the shower toward her. As soon as I'm close enough, I wrap the bottom of her shirt around my hand.

"Wait!"

I freeze, the way her voice shakes on the word pulling me up short.

"Um, I need to say something before you take my clothes off," she whispers, tilting her head back against the wall. Her eyes are dilated, her cheeks flushed. I don't think her color is from the cold this time though. My magical little elf is turned on.

"You can tell me anything," I promise when she hesitates.

"If this is going where I think it's going, um, you should know that I've neverhadsexbefore," she says all in a rush, like she doesn't want me to hear her.

I chuckle at how cute she is.

"I know."

"You do?" Her head tilts to the side again, her gaze turning suspicious. "How do you know?"

"Because," I murmur, tugging her shirt up her gorgeous body. "A man would have to be a complete moron to get this close to you and then let you go. And men may not always be smart, but we're not crazy. There's not a fucking chance one would have let you get away after getting inside you."

"Oh," she whispers.

I grin, slipping my free hand under her shirt to touch her stomach. Her skin is still chilled, but it's warming up. She's so damn soft.

"You have the power here, little elf," I murmur. "If all you want to share with me is a shower and a few kisses, I'm okay with that."

"Okay." She nibbles her bottom lip, and then tilts her heart-shaped face up to mine again. With the steam swirling around her, she looks like a water nymph. "What if I want to share more than that, Sawyer?"

"Then I'll be the luckiest man on the planet."

Her bright smile saps all the moisture from my mouth. "I think I'll be pretty lucky too; you know. You're so incredible. Spending today with you is already one of my favorite Christmas memories."

Jesus, this woman. This sweet, beautiful, brilliant woman.

I never knew falling in love would be so effortless or happen so fast. I always thought it took time and growing pains and those little moments in between where everything slowly comes together to reveal the bigger picture. It's not at all like that. I think it happened the first time she smiled at me. Or maybe when she jumped right in and decided I was going to spend Christmas with her. I'm not sure. But my heart is in her capable little hands and I feel nothing but joy.

I tug her shirt up and pull it off over her head, letting it drop beside mine. My gaze roves over her, taking in every dip and curve on her body. My god, she is a vision in her little black bra with candy canes and mistletoe printed all over it.

I run my hands all over her, listening to the way her breath speeds, watching how her skin pebbles in response to my touch. She truly is soft and sweet everywhere.

"It's going to take a miracle to get these leggings off," she warns me when I reach for them.

I kneel in front of her. Together, we shimmy them down her legs. I have to fight to keep from burying my face in her center. Like her bra, her panties are covered in candy canes and mistletoe. Why that's so sexy to me, I don't know, but it is. The way she throws her whole heart into everything is so damn beautiful.

She is beautiful, a pale winter star shining bright enough to eclipse even the sun.

"Lift your foot," I murmur once we finally manage to peel her leggings down.

She places a hand on my shoulder and does as instructed, allowing me to pull them the rest of the way off one leg and then the other. I toss them aside and then sit there for a moment, just staring at her in awe.

She stares back, her eyes wide and dark with desire.

"You're the most beautiful little elf I've ever seen, Lana. Jesus, you have no idea what you do to me, do you?" I ask, rising to my feet again. I wrap a hand around her waist, pulling her body up against mine. My lips touch hers.

"Show me," she whispers.

CHAPTER SIX

LANA

"**S**awyer," I moan, trembling as he backs me up against the shower wall with his hands around my waist. His lips are locked on mine, his kisses hot enough to make lava jealous. My entire body hums with desire like I've never felt before. He's barely even touched me and I'm already aching with need.

"Lana," he whispers against my lips before breaking away to kiss a trail down my chest. He slips the straps of my bra down, kissing each shoulder and then the swells of my breasts. His body brackets mine. With steam swirling around us and water falling inside and out, it feels like we're in our own little world, completely separate from everyone and everything else.

I lean forward so he can reach the clasp on my bra. He manages to undo it a lot faster than I managed to get it done this morning. As soon as he slides the straps down my arms, my bra joins the pile of soaked clothes in the corner.

He wraps one hand around my waist, securing me against him. The other runs between my breasts and then over the right. His palm gently abrades my nipple, making me moan his name again. I never imagined such tender caresses could feel so heavenly, but they do.

"Steady, little star," he croons, his lips chasing mine again.

I loop my arms around his neck, drag my hands over his broad shoulders as he kisses me hard and deep. He is so darn big and strong. I've never met anyone like him, who is so wholly perfect inside and out. The way he loves his family is beautiful. *He* is beautiful, a sturdy oak standing firm in a fierce winter storm.

How could I not tumble headfirst into love with him? He is infinitely, fiercely deserving of it. There was no question of giving him my heart. He stole it without even trying. I think he might have claimed it when I first heard him laugh. Or perhaps he took it when he let me bulldoze my way into his life and his home.

The hand on my waist slips down my belly. His fingers tease at the waistband of my panties. All of my muscles clench in anticipation of his touch. I want it, ache for it. I'm certainly not cold anymore. All I feel is desire, licking like flames all over my body.

"Has anyone ever touched you before, sweet Lana?" he asks.

"No."

"Good." His little boy grin is full of possessive pride. "I like knowing I'm going to be the first one to have any part of you."

I like knowing that too. A lot. He's the only man I've ever wanted to have this part of me. Even if he never learns to love me too, I'll cherish this memory of him for the rest of my life.

"Father Christmas," I gasp when he slips his hand inside my panties and runs a finger across my slit. A powerful jolt of pleasure rips through me. "That feels good."

"It'll feel a whole lot better soon," he says. The promise reflects in his eyes. He keeps his gaze locked on my face as he touches me, watching what he does to me.

I watch him too, fascinated at how much he seems to enjoy giving me pleasure. The way his eyes darken until they're almost black is sexy. So is the pleased sound he makes when I tilt my head back against the wall and cry out his name.

He explores every little part of me with his fingers, finding sensitive places that send more jolts of pleasure through me. There are so many of them. Jeez. I never knew this could feel so good. I've touched myself before, but it didn't feel like this, as if every nerve ending is being caressed all at once.

His thumb grinds against my clit and I lose eye contact with him. My head thumps against the wall, my legs trembling beneath me. He makes another of those sexy sounds and drops to his knees in front of me. He's less gentle as he rips my panties down my legs and tosses them aside.

"I need to taste you," he says, his voice a gritty rasp of sound I feel in my core. He wraps one big hand around my calf, lifting my leg to drape it over his shoulder. His eyes meet mine again, burning with need. "Hold on to me."

I barely have time to grasp his shoulders before he wraps one arm around my waist to pull me closer. He uses the other to open me up to him. My cheeks burn to have him looking at me down there, but then he grits out a curse and my embarrassment disappears.

"Christ, you're soft and pink everywhere," he growls, leaning in. He runs his lips up my thigh, setting off a chain reaction of little detonations inside me. When he sinks his teeth into my inner thigh, a bigger detonation explodes in my veins, turning my blood to liquid fire. He buries his face in my center. His tongue swipes through my folds and dances around my clit.

"Sawyer!" I cry out, dazed.

"I knew you'd taste like candy," he growls. He doesn't give me time to say anything before he turns into a hungry beast. His hold on me tightens and he eats me like a little boy in a candy store. His lips and tongue and teeth drive me crazy, setting off detonation after detonation, until I'm sobbing his name because the pleasure just builds and builds and then builds some more.

His tongue runs around my clit in circles before he dips lower and pushes the tip of it into me. He jiggles it there, growling as he tries to push it in deeper. My nails embed themselves in his shoulder blades, his name leaving my lips in a high-pitched chant as the detonations of pleasure suddenly turn inward. They no longer explode in my veins but pile on top of one another deep inside my belly.

"Fuck, this little thing is so tight and sweet. I can't wait to feel you wrapped around my cock," Sawyer says before attacking my clit again. He slips one finger inside me and then another, pushing and twisting and thrusting. His lips seam around my clit and he curls his fingers up to touch some magical spot inside me.

All those stalled detonations go off at once, exploding like a wall of pleasure slamming into me. It's savage in its intensity, so much more powerful than anything I've ever felt before. I scream his name as it launches me into orbit. I come hard, lights bursting behind my eyelids in a whirling kaleidoscope of color.

Sawyer eats me through it, growling and snarling. He's rough and possessive but so gentle at the same time as he guides me through it, crooning my name. The sound of his voice grounds my soul while the rest of me flies to heaven.

And then he eases me back down to earth with sweet kisses to my clit and soft praises that have tears stinging my eyes. It's perfect. He's perfect.

"Come on, sweet Lana," he croons when I finally land back in his arms, as safe as houses. He turns the shower off and reaches out to grab another towel.

My body trembles as he dries me off. Even the fluffy towel against my overheated skin feels like sensory overload.

As soon as I'm dry, he quickly yanks his boxers off and dries himself. Before I can get a good look at him, he scoops me up into his arms. My head lolls against his shoulder as he strides through the bathroom with me and then into his bedroom to lay me out on the bed. It's soft as a cloud.

Rain still sheets down outside, blotting out our view of the city.

"Sweet, sweet Lana," Sawyer whispers, following me down. His hard body covers mine. He brushes my hair back from my face, raining kisses across my cheeks and eyelids. "My perfect little star."

I tilt my face up to his, greedy for more of his kisses.

He chuckles and gives them to me, teasing me with his tongue and little bites to my bottom lip. I taste myself on him, taste the way our flavors mingle. I'm not sure if I'm supposed to like it or not, but there's something erotic and naughty about tasting myself on him.

His erection nudges at my belly.

I reach for him blindly, eager to get my hands on him.

"Fuck," he groans when I brush my hand across the head of his cock. Moisture wets the tip, sliding down my knuckles. He's so hard and yet so soft at the same time. He's also a lot bigger than I expected. Then again, the rest of him is big and hard too. I guess it only makes sense for this part to be the same way.

I explore him with my fingers, loving the way he pants for breath and moans as I trail my fingers down the underside of his cock and then drag them up the thick vein that runs the length of it. I try to fit my hand around him but can't. His balls are nestled in a tight thatch of curls.

"Christ, you're killing me," he growls when I cup them in my hand and then roll them between my fingers. He bites my lip again, an impatient, greedy nip.

I love it.

"Make love to me, Sawyer," I whisper, stroking him from root to tip. I'm not really sure what I'm doing or if I'm doing it right, but he seems to like it.

His breath rasps in his throat and his big body trembles over mine.

"I want you inside me."

"God, little star," he moans, reaching for my hand.

He pulls it away from his erection, tangling our fingers up together. He grabs the other one and does the same thing, pinning them to the bed on each side of my head.

I don't feel trapped or vulnerable beneath him though. He's powerfully strong, but I have the power here. He's all alpha, but he's also mine to command. I think, if I wanted to do it, I could probably rule him with a single word.

"Shit."

"What?"

"I don't have a condom," he murmurs, meeting my gaze. His eyes rove over my face, his expression so fierce and serious. "Not sure I'd want to wear one with you even if I did have one, sweet girl. I want to feel all of you."

"I..." I should tell him we need a condom, but I don't want to be responsible and safe with him. I want to be reckless and wild and throw every part of me into loving him. "What if I get pregnant?"

"You think I wouldn't be the happiest man alive?" He arches a brow, hitting me with a look so hot, I'm pretty sure the bed just caught fire. "If you want babies, you're having mine, Lana. No one else's." He dips his head until his lips are at my ear. "I can't wait to see you with my babies."

"I...I want that," I whisper the truth, my voice shaking at the thought of having this beautiful man's babies. That he wants it too gives me hope that he feels the same way I do...that we share the same sense of comfortable inevitability, as if what's between us was always meant to happen.

We were both at the school last night for a reason, and not for the seemingly mundane ones we gave, but because we felt compelled to be there for reasons neither of us could explain. I could have dropped off the equipment today or any other day. But I didn't. He could have unpacked his office any other day. But he didn't. I think we chose last night because we were supposed to be there.

I've always believed in the magic of Christmas, believed that extraordinary things happen this time of year, more so than at any other time. I think I was right.

He's my extraordinary thing. My magic.

"Sawyer?" I whisper, my heart racing.

"Yeah, little star?"

"I love you."

His eyes meet mine, his lashes fluttering. The look of awe on his face, of joy...God, I want to see it there every day of forever. "You love me?"

"So much," I whisper, tears trembling in my lashes.

His forehead touches mine, a soft sigh washing across my face. "Sweet little star," he whispers reverently, his lips resting against mine. "I gave you my heart the first time I heard you laugh. I'm so hopelessly, ridiculously, happily in love with you."

"Me too."

He kisses me so sweetly the tears trembling in my lashes slip down my cheeks. We get lost in each other, in the powerful connection between us and the magic in the very air around us.

He nudges my leg with his thigh, silently demanding that I open up for him.

I give him what he wants, draping one leg over his thigh.

"Kris Kringle," I gasp, arching upward when his erection grinds against my clit. "That feels way better than when I touch myself."

"Jesus. Even when I'm about to fuck you senseless, you still make me laugh," he says, burying his face in my throat as his body shakes with laughter. "How many Christmas curses do you have in you?"

"A lot." I run my hands up and down his back, touching him everywhere I can reach. I love the way his muscles feel beneath my palms. They bunch and ripple as if responding to the feel of my hands on his body. "I've been saving them up all year."

He laughs again and then kisses my throat. "I fucking love them. You can use them anywhere you want, but when we're in this bed, the only name you say is mine, Lana."

"Okay," I agree because he sounds all possessive and bossy. And also because I really love saying his name. "Sawyer? I really need you inside me now, please."

"Yes, ma'am." He chuckles and then his grip tightens on my hands.

He grinds himself against my clit, seeking out my mouth. The kiss starts off slow and soft, tinged with sweetness, but it quickly grows hotter, wilder. As easily as we laugh together, we burn together. He rocks his hips against me, running his erection over my clit again and again, making me crazy. I'm so wet I feel it on my thighs.

My breath stalls in my lungs when he notches himself at my entrance.

"I love you," he whispers, thrusting forward. My body stretches around him. It's an odd sensation but it doesn't hurt. Even when the head of his erection finally slips in, I don't feel pain.

That changes when he grits his teeth and surges forward again. He tries to be gentle, but I still feel it when my hymen tears. The sting ripples through me, making me whimper and dig my nails into his upper arms.

"Breathe, sweet Lana," he croons, kissing me between each word. "Keep breathing, little star." He holds himself still inside me, his muscles locked tight. His breath rasps out of his throat, strangled. "God, I can't believe you're real. You feel like heaven around me." His nose glides along the side of mine before he kisses away the tears pooling in my eyes. "You're my miracle, my bright little star. I'm never going to let you go now that I found you."

"G-good," I whisper. Even though it shouldn't be possible, awe courses through me almost as strongly as the pain does. He loves me. He's inside me. Somehow, this is really my life. This beautiful man is mine and I don't ever have to give him back.

His lips brush my forehead and linger. "Thank you for bringing her to me, God," he whispers so softly I'm not sure the words are meant for my ears.

I hear them anyway.

They make me cry anyway.

"I love you."

"I love you, sweet Lana." His lips chase mine again, our kiss steeped in emotion and tinged with the taste of my tears. For long moments, all we do is kiss and cling to one another, both brought to our knees with gratitude and love. And then he shifts his hips.

I gasp as pain gives way to pleasure.

"Sorry, little star. Sorry," he apologizes, misunderstanding.

"Sawyer," I breathe against his lips. "Do that again, please. Make love to me."

"You're sure?"

"Positive."

He tilts his hips forward just a bit, testing. When I moan his name, he relaxes and surges forward, filling me completely. His head tips back, a decadent groan rippling in the air around us, though I'm not sure if it came from him or from me.

He lets go of my hands to plant his on the bed beside my head.

"There's no way I'm ever going to get enough of you," he says, gliding in and out of me in slow strokes before he picks up speed. His body rocks above mine, his chest brushing across my breasts with every move. "You're so damn perfect, Lana. Jesus."

"So are you." I run my hands down his back, throwing my head back and moaning. God, having him inside me feels so *damn* good. Like I've found exactly where I belong.

He dips his head, pulling my nipple into his mouth...and it gets even better.

I cry out his name, using my hands on his ass to pull him closer. He takes the hint and thrusts harder, impaling me on him over and over again. Each time our bodies come together, his balls smack against my bottom, leaving a little sting. Even that feels good.

He moves from breast to breast, licking and sucking, leaving little love bites in his wake. A steady stream of curses and praise fall from his lips, some so dirty they make me blush, others so sweet they make me want to cry.

The bed squeaks beneath me as he makes love to me, moving from place to place on my body as if he knows every sensitive area that I have. I leave claw marks in his firm ass and back, sob his name into the room.

Pleasure is an endless well rising up to consume me again and then again. Sweat glides down my skin and makes a sheen on his. He's a warrior above me, pounding into me and groaning my name as if he can't help but say it when we're like this. He gives it to me over and over again.

"Lana. Lana. God, little star," he groans, tilting my hips and striking a spot inside me that makes me see stars. "What are you doing to me?"

"L-loving you," I gasp, arching beneath him, writhing, twisting to get closer and to make him go even deeper. I touch him like he did me, seeking out every spot on his body that makes him tremble and gasp my name.

He growls when I reach between us, wanting to feel where we're connected. I'm so wet and he's so hard. We fit together like we were made to be like this, to love like this. My fingertips trail down the root of him and then whisper across his balls.

"Fuck," he curses, grabbing for my hand.

Before I can even complain or say anything, he has both of my arms over my head, holding me down again. His eyes blaze with heat and wicked intention. He takes me hard then, pounding into me in relentless strikes that have me sobbing his name and babbling to the heavens.

My belly quickens and blooms for him.

"That's it," he growls, nipping at my throat. "Give me what belongs to me. I want it." He thrusts deep and circles his hips so the root of him grinds against my clit. Again and then again.

"Sawyer," I sob, writhing as the orgasm takes me. It's frightfully powerful, as fierce as the storm still raging outside. It crashes over me like a tidal wave, drowning me in pleasure. I shout his name, crying it into the room until it echoes around us.

He impales me on him, his drives ruthless as he fucks me right out of this world and leaves me suspended in some peaceful, perfect place where the only thing that exists is pleasure...and him.

"Lana!" he roars as he loses his rhythm and begins to spill inside me. His groan rolls over me like a second orgasm, sending aftershocks through me. I feel warmth as he finds release, filling me full of him. It's warm and sticky, messy and perfect.

I love it. I love him.

"Lana," he breathes, collapsing partially on top of me when it's finally over. He holds his weight off me, careful not to crush me as we both pant for breath and tremble in the aftermath. His body shelters mine, all that fierce strength and gentle devotion wrapped tightly around me. "I love you."

I don't know if miracles exist...but I think he might be mine.

"I love you," he whispers again, seeking out my lips.

I offer them up to him willingly, without reservation. The same way I gave him my heart.

CHAPTER SEVEN

SAWYER

"With a corn cob pipe and a butt and nose," I sing along to the radio with Lana.

"And two ey—Sawyer!" she cries mid-word, her body shaking with laughter. "It's *button nose*, not *butt and nose*!"

"Close enough," I mutter, grinning at her. She's so damn beautiful when she's happy. The storm ended a few hours ago, and she dragged me out of bed to finish her cookies. We spent the afternoon cuddling in the kitchen while she baked, and our clothes dried.

Now the cookies are all delivered, and her overnight bag is in the back seat of my truck. I'm dying to get her home and back in bed. My little elf is spending the night with me before we go to her mom's for Christmas tomorrow. She wanted to introduce us at the hospital, but her mom was in the operating room.

I'm looking forward to meeting her. I hope like hell she thinks I'm worthy of her little girl because I'm not giving Lana back. I want my ring on her finger and her name tied to mine as quickly as humanly possible.

"You're terrible at Christmas music," Lana says, still laughing as we coast to a stop at the sign a block from the house.

"You'll just have to teach me to do better then, little star."

She beams at me before throwing her head back and belting out the next verse in that angelic voice of hers. She really is my little star, lighting up my world with a simple smile. I never knew dimples could be so irresistible. I can't remember the last time I felt this, this...*free.*

I turn onto our street, chuckling as she sings my lyrics this time with a mischievous grin and a soft laugh that rings like music throughout the truck.

My laughter dies as soon as the house comes into view.

"What the fuck?" I frown at the SUV parked in the driveway beside Lana's Malibu, my heart pounding. Anxiety claws inside my stomach, twisting like a knife.

"What's wrong?" Lana follows my gaze and then her brows furrow when she spots the Acadia parked in the driveway. "Who is it, Sawyer?"

"My family," I say around the lump in my throat. "It's my family."

Lana reaches for my hand, squeezing it in hers. "They missed you," she whispers, her voice soft. "And they love you."

"I know," I rasp, bringing her hand to my lips to brush a grateful kiss across her knuckles. I pull in behind my dad's SUV and park.

"You deserve your spot in their lives," Lana reminds me when I make no move to get out. "And they deserve their place in yours. That's why they're here."

The doors on the SUV open and Savannah pops out, waving wildly. She's bundled up in a pink parka like we live in Alaska, little more than her cherubic face and flashes of her dark hair visible beneath the furry hood. A second later, Saint climbs out behind her. He's less exuberant as he steps up beside her.

He looks different...good. His hair is longer. His beard is neatly trimmed. He's packed on muscle. His usual smirk and confidence are gone. In its place is a quiet reserve and hesitation I've never seen from him before.

Saint has always been loud and full of life. People love him because he's always teasing and having a good time. He's a practical joker and has been his entire life. As a kid, he was forever in trouble because he couldn't sit still. He spent more time causing mischief than anything else.

He lifts his head, meeting my gaze. It might be my imagination, but I think he swallows. Even in the fading light, I can see the shame and guilt burning in his eyes. He looks at me as if he's afraid to face me. That kills me a little.

How the hell did we get here? I can't help but wonder.

How the hell did we both get so fucking lost?

"I can distract them if you need a minute," Lana says, compassion brimming in her voice. And I know she'd do it. She'd hop out and face my family on her own to give me a minute to pull myself together and rebuild the walls she sent tumbling today.

This magical little elf would usher them inside and ease my way without hesitation if I asked it of her. She would be brave and strong and let me retreat back behind the barriers I've put up between myself and my family. And she'd do it without once casting judgement or feeling disappointment.

For the thousandth time since I met her, I fall in love with her.

"I'm good, little star," I murmur, her quiet acceptance giving me the courage I need. Her love giving me the strength to let the last of those walls collapse into ruin. Just that easily...I let it go.

I turn the truck off as my mom and dad climb from the SUV, waiting patiently for me to come to them.

"Wait for me."

Lana nods her agreement, watching me carefully as I climb from the truck and circle around to help her down. My family watches in silence as I lift her from the truck and slide her down my body. I can practically feel Savannah and my mom's excitement though. I've never wanted to introduce a woman to my family, but I can't wait to claim this one in front of them.

Once my little star is on her feet, I grab her bag from the back. She's putting up a brave front, but I can tell she's nervous to meet my family. I brush strands of hair back from her face and smile at her before tangling our hands together.

"I love you," I remind her.

Her expression melts and I know she's okay with meeting them here and now.

As soon as I shut the truck door, Savannah pounces.

"Surprise!" she yells, shuffling forward to fling her arms around me. "I missed you so much!"

I release Lana's hand long enough to squeeze Savannah as tightly as I dare.

"I missed you too, brat," I whisper in her ear, my throat tight with emotion. "I'm so sorry for everything I've missed."

"I know you are," she whispers back. "Please give him a chance. He misses you."

"I know." I swallow and admit the truth. "I miss him too."

Savannah's hug turns fierce before she finally releases me. Pandemonium ensues as I introduce her and Lana and then my mom and dad come forward to say hello and meet my girl. My mom looks like she's ready to break out in a happy dance. So does Savannah.

My dad is more reserved as he pats me on the back. "She's beautiful, son."

"She's perfect," I correct, which makes him laugh.

Lana takes charge of my mom and Savannah, demanding my keys so she can let them in to pee. They're not even halfway up the driveway before they're all chattering back and forth a million miles a minute. I'm not surprised. I knew my family would love Lana. It's impossible not to love her.

Lana stops long enough to throw her arms around Saint in a big hug. He stumbles back a step, no doubt shocked by her quick acceptance, and then his expression cracks and he pulls her in to hug her tightly. I think she says something to him because his eyes come to me and he nods.

"I'll give you two a minute," Dad says before taking off after the girls when Lana releases Saint and he takes a step in my direction.

Dad murmurs something to him as he walks past.

Saint jerks his chin in a nod but doesn't respond.

For a long time after the front door closes, we just stand in the driveway, looking at each other. It's awkward as hell. Flashes of the last time I saw him play through my mind. The two of us rolling around on the ground, fists and heated words flying. Saint's broken nose. My bloody lip. The cops prying us apart and throwing him in the back of a squad car.

"I can find a hotel if you don't want me here," he finally says, scrubbing a hand through his hair. He takes another halting step in my direction. "I wouldn't blame you if you didn't. I fucked up. I know I fucked up."

"Yeah, you did," I agree, my voice soft.

He flinches.

"But so did I." I expel a breath and move toward him. "I said things I didn't mean because I was pissed at myself for not wanting to admit how bad your drinking had gotten. I've always looked out for you and Savannah. It killed me that I didn't protect the two of you like I should have."

"I didn't want you to know how bad it was," he says. "I didn't want to be a fucking disappointment to you again."

"You've never been a disappointment, Saint." I shake my head, my heart in my throat that he could think that. "I've always been proud as hell of you. Didn't always agree with the stunts you pulled or the things you did, but I was never anything less than proud to call you my brother."

"I know you don't believe me, but I wasn't drinking that day. I was hungover, but I was sober." He swallows hard. "I never would have let her ride with me if I'd had a drink. I may do a lot of stupid, reckless shit, but I would never risk her life like that."

"You're serious," I say, reading it on his face.

He nods.

"You let everyone believe you were drinking."

"There was whiskey all over the car. Even had I denied it, no one would have believed me." He meets my gaze and swallows hard, shoving his hands into his pockets. "You didn't."

"Jesus Christ," I whisper, stunned.

"I deserved what I got. Whether I was drunk or not, the wreck was still my fault," he says, glancing away from me. He clenches his jaw. "She almost died because I was a reckless fucking idiot who thought I had everything under control when I didn't." A pained bark of laughter erupts from between his lips. It sounds more like a broken sob. "I hadn't been in control in a long fucking time, man."

"Jesus," I whisper, striding forward to pull him into a hug.

He resists for a long moment, his muscles locked tight. And then he hugs me back. "I'm sorry," he rasps, his entire body shaking. "I'm so fucking sorry, Sawyer."

"It's over, Saint," I promise him, tears in my eyes as he breaks down, purging himself of a year of grief and regret. I had a magical little star to help me through mine. It's only right that I help get him through his. He's my brother, my best friend. I want him back in my life.

"It's time to let it go and move on," I tell him. "For both of us."

"Hey," Lana says, reaching for my hand when Saint and I finally make it inside. We didn't say much else. Hell, there wasn't much else to say. My girl was right. We can both cling to what happened and let it destroy us or we can let it go and move on. I want to move on...and I want the same thing for my brother.

The fact that he never tried to defend himself because he didn't think anyone would believe him...because *I* didn't believe him...never again. That won't happen ever again. I can't change the past, but I can make sure he doesn't go through shit like that alone in the future.

"Hey." I pull Lana into my arms, holding her tight.

Her arms go around me, and she squeezes as if she's trying to put me back together through sheer physical will again. Only, I'm not in pieces this time.

"Are you okay?" she asks.

"Yeah," I promise, pressing my lips to her forehead. "I'm good now. We're good now."

She tips her head back to examine my face. Whatever she sees there makes her smile and flash those dimples at me like I just pulled the moon down and handed it to her. Her happiness for me is soul deep.

How soon is too soon to marry her?

"My family behaving themselves?" I ask her, earning a loud protest from Savannah.

"I want to keep them," Lana whispers, making me laugh.

"Of course you do." I kiss her hard on the mouth and then turn to greet my family. They're all sitting around my kitchen, plates of cookies spread out on the table around them. Even Saint has taken a seat...and a small pile of cookies that he's inhaling in single bites.

Seeing him here...having all of them here...it's good. It's better than good. For the first time since the accident, I feel like I deserve to be here with them. I feel like I deserve *them*.

"Family, meet my soon-to-be wife," I murmur, turning Lana to face them with a smile on my face. "Soon-to-be wife, meet your soon-to-be in-laws."

Savannah squeals.

Lana squeaks and spins right back around to face me, her eyes comically wide. "Son of a nutcracker, Sawyer!" she whisper-shouts. "You can't tell your family we're getting married the first time I meet them! They'll think I'm crazy."

"Sweetheart, if you're marrying him, you are crazy," my dad drawls.

"Amar, you hush!" My mom laughs and swats him on the shoulder. I can tell by the giant smile on her face that she's thrilled by the news. I can also tell she already loves my girl. Which means I'm going to have to be sneaky if I want any time alone with her because my mom will absolutely shiv me in the ribs for girl time with Lana. She's kind of terrifying.

"He's just joking," Lana says, her face scrunched up in the cutest little scowl.

"The hell I am," I growl, cocking a brow at her. "We're getting married, little star."

"You haven't even asked me."

"Do you want to marry me?"

She purses her lips and pretends to think about it. "I mean, since Chris Hemsworth isn't available, I guess so."

She squeals and tries to escape when I growl again and lunge for her.

"I'm kidding! I'm kidding!" she cries through laughter when I catch her, dragging her back into my arms. "I'd marry you even if Chris Hemsworth was available."

I kiss her hard on the mouth, not giving a shit if my family is watching every move we make. This little elf is mine. She's marrying me, end of discussion.

"I'm getting a sister!" Savannah shouts. "This is the best Christmas ever!"

She's right. It is the best Christmas ever.

CHAPTER EIGHT

LANA

"I'm so happy for you, baby girl," Mom says, hugging me tight as we say goodbye at the front door on Christmas night. Instead of us going to her, she came to us for Christmas. It made more sense than trying to cram all of us into her small apartment. Even Aunt Leslie came for dinner.

Sawyer's family left a couple hours ago to make the drive back home. I guess this was a last-minute trip, plotted by Savannah and Celeste, his mom. His dad has an important meeting the day after tomorrow. They didn't want Sawyer spending Christmas alone though, so they came to him.

Seeing him with them made me so happy. The love they share is incredible. I didn't ask for details about what happened between him and Saint, but I think they're in a better place now. They've spent the day bonding over football and teasing Savannah. It's obvious they both dote on her. It's also clear that she idolizes them both.

Savannah and I are going to be great friends, I know it. She's such a sweet girl, wise and compassionate beyond her years. What she went through may have left scars on her body, but it didn't leave a single mark on her heart. She loves fiercely.

I think my mom and Sawyer's mom are already best friends. They're already ganging up on Sawyer to badger him about giving them time to plan a real wedding. He told them that I could have whatever I wanted, so long as it could be done by the end of the year.

We could get married anywhere and I would be happy. All I want is to be his, and to have our families there with us. That's all I need.

His family is going to drive back up later this week so they can be here when we get married.

I can't believe I'm getting married! People might think we're crazy for jumping in with both feet, but that's all right because I know we're not. What's between us is powerful and it's right.

"I'm happy for me too," I whisper to my mom.

"He's a good man."

"He's the best man."

She laughs quietly and releases me. "I guess we're not going to the gym in the morning?"

"Um, I'm not sure." We always go to the gym the day after Christmas to work off what we ate, but I hate the gym and kind of want to spend the morning in bed with Sawyer. I slept so peacefully in his arms all night.

"Trust me, honey, with the way that man was looking at you all day, you're not going to the gym in the morning," she says, wiggling her brows at me. Her green eyes shine with humor.

"Mom!"

"I'm just saying!" She laughs loudly and then kisses me on the cheek. "Call me tomorrow, baby girl. We'll go to the gym another day. I love you."

"I love you too, Mom. Merry Christmas."

She kisses me again and then heads out to her car. Sawyer and Saint carried all of her stuff out for her before Saint left so she didn't have to carry anything. Saint is nothing like I thought he would be. I expected the wild rockstar I read about, but he's really down to earth and kind of quiet and sweet. I guess what happened changed him as much as it did Sawyer. He may have lost his way for a while, but I think he's a good man, one worthy of as much love as Sawyer is. I hope he finds peace. He deserves it.

I stand at the door and watch until mom backs down the driveway and heads out. Once her taillights disappear, I lock up and go in search of Sawyer. I stop in the living room to straighten up the cushions on the sofa. We managed to get most of the first floor unpacked and put away between opening gifts and cooking. It didn't take long with everyone pitching in to help.

I fluff the pillows and then scoop up an empty cookie plate from the coffee table before heading to the kitchen. Our moms pretty much took it over today to cook for everyone. Savannah and I helped with the baking before we joined the men at the table to play cards. Savanah totally cheats at Uno, and Sawyer is terrible at Phase Ten. Their dad was probably a card shark in a past life. He is ruthless, and he won almost every game. Saint was really good too.

It was the best Christmas.

The kitchen is already clean, but I start the dishwasher and wipe down the cabinets before turning off the lights and going to find my man. I don't know where he disappeared to this time.

He snuck out this morning to go shopping for me. I don't know how he found anything open on Christmas, but he managed to do it. I felt bad because I didn't have anything to give him or his family, but he took care of that too. He's kind of perfect.

I head upstairs in search of him, and then pause outside the bedroom door when I hear him singing from inside in his deep baritone. He's making up his own lyrics again. I think I might like his versions better than the originals just because they're his.

I love everything about him.

When I step inside the bedroom, I don't see him. Lights flicker in the bathroom and music trickles out into the bedroom.

"Sawyer?" I head that way.

"Stay right there!" he yells from inside. "Don't even think about coming in here."

"Why not?" I yell back, smiling. He's so bossy sometimes.

"Because I said so!"

"Bossy," I mumble, laughing. I don't really mind. It's kind of hot when he gets all growly and bossy and tries to tell me what to do. I only listen because I know it makes him happy. I also know that if I really wanted in there, he wouldn't try to stop me. He hasn't told me no since we met.

Instead of ruining whatever surprise he's working on in there, I jump up onto the bed and then lay down, staring out at the city. With the lights on, I can't really see anything but my own reflection. I look happy.

I *am* happy. The way Sawyer makes me feel...I've never felt anything like it before. I've always been content with my life, but it's never been this soul-deep sense of satisfaction that has seeped into every pore and sunk deep into every bone. That's all Sawyer's doing.

My hand rests on my stomach, which makes my smile grow. I don't know if it's possible to will yourself pregnant, but I wish it with every fiber of my being anyway. The thought of having kids with Sawyer makes me ache with longing. I want that more than I ever dreamed possible, little boys with his beautiful brown eyes and mischievous smile. Maybe even a little girl who looks like me.

"Wake up, little star." Something soft drifts down the side of my face.

I blink my eyes open to find Sawyer standing over me, smiling. He runs his hand down the side of my face again, looking at me with so much love in his eyes that it makes my heart flutter and race. How did I get lucky enough to find this beautiful man?

"Did I fall asleep?"

"Mmhmm," he hums. "But it's time to wake up now. I have a surprise for you."

"I like surprises."

"I know you do." He chuckles and then leans down to scoop me up into his arms.

I think he likes carrying me around. He does it at every available opportunity. I don't mind. I love feeling his arms around me and all of those muscles working to keep me safe. Letting him carry me doesn't worry me at all. I have no reservations about being in his arms. It's my favorite place.

"Close your eyes," he whispers, tipping his head down to brush a kiss across my lips. His hair falls forward to tickle my forehead.

My eyes flutter closed.

He carries me into the bathroom and then places me on my feet, wrapping his arms around me from behind. I sway in his arms, humming when he sweeps my hair to the side to run his lips up the side of my throat. The entire bathroom smells like a winter oasis—notes of vanilla, cranberry, and cinnamon mingling in the air.

"Open your eyes, sweet girl," Sawyer whispers in my ear.

"Oh my goodness," I breathe, staring in awe at the bathroom.

Candlelight reflects back like thousands of flickering stars caught in the glass shower wall and the mirrors. They rest on every surface. Strands of white Christmas lights hang over the mirrors, filling the room with a soft glow. Red and white rose petals are scattered around the floor and float on the fragrant bubbles practically overflowing the tub. He's set up a little tray across part of it with wine and chocolate dipped strawberries on top. Somehow, he's even put up a little Christmas tree beside the tub and decorated it.

"Merry Christmas," he whispers, pressing his lips to my temple.

"Sawyer," I turn around in his arms, my heart swelling with emotion that sends tears into my eyes. "I can't believe you did all of this for me."

"Sweet, sweet Lana." His tender smile sends two tears down my cheeks. "This is the least you deserve for everything you've done for me. You gave me hope and my family back. You made today perfect. God, little star. You've made my life so much better since I met you."

"Sawyer," I sob.

He chuckles at me and then cups my cheeks in his hands to thumb away my tears. "No crying, sweet girl. I want you to relax and let me pamper you for a little while. You haven't stopped moving all day."

"Will you get in with me?"

"I will." His lips touch mine in a sweet kiss. He tries to pull back without deepening it, but I throw my arms around his neck and kiss him with every fiber of my being. He growls and clutches me to him, kissing me like he's been starving for the taste of me. He wanted to make love to me again last night, but I was afraid his parents would hear us from their room next door.

Somehow, we manage to undress between long kisses. He does most of the work. I'm too blissed out in love with him to be much help. He doesn't seem to mind. As soon as we're both naked, he wraps his hand around mine to lead me to the tub.

I come to a dead stop when I see what I missed earlier. A tiny box sits beneath the tree.

"Is that–?"

"For you? All of this is for you, little star." He nudges me gently. "Take it."

I stumble forward on shaking legs to scoop up the box wrapped neatly in red and green paper, my heart in my throat. Sawyer watches with one of those little boy smiles as I carefully slice through the paper. I'm not sure if my hands are trembling or if it's my whole body, but I almost drop the box twice before I finally get the wrapping paper off it.

It's a ring box.

"Sawyer," I whisper, stunned. "How did you do this?"

"Saint called in every favor he's owed to find a jeweler willing to let me in at dawn," he murmurs, taking the box from my hands. He takes the wrapping paper too and tosses it toward the trashcan. "I couldn't stand the thought of another night falling without you wearing my ring."

"I can't believe you bought me a ring on Christmas," I whisper, awe and adoration crashing through me. No one has ever gone to such lengths for me before. That he did makes me want to throw my arms around him and never, ever let go.

"I would have given it to you earlier, but I wanted this memory to be about just me and you," he says. He sinks to his knee in front of me. Even naked on his knee with rose petals all around him, he's the strongest, most fiercely beautiful man I've ever met...and the sweetest. "C'mere, sweet girl."

I stumble forward a few steps.

He flips the ring box open between us. I gasp as soon as I see it. The center stone is a giant square cut emerald. Two round diamonds sit on each side in the center of little lotus-like flowers. The platinum band splits into two sections on each side, all four delicate pieces lined with smaller diamonds. It's unique and incredibly beautiful. I instantly fall in love with it.

"Yes," I whisper.

"You didn't let me ask," Sawyer says, chuckling. He doesn't seem to mind though. He slips the ring out of the box and onto my finger. It fits perfectly. Somehow, I'm not surprised.

He's so freaking amazing.

Aunt Leslie promised me that the school board wouldn't interfere with us being together. She said they couldn't do a whole lot about it, especially since Sebastian married Rowan and they didn't fire him. I hope she's right because I'm not giving Sawyer up now that he's mine.

"Jack Frost," he whispers, reverence in his voice as he looks at the ring on my finger and then at me. "I like seeing you in nothing but my ring, Lana. You're really marrying me?"

"I am."

His eyes meet mine, blazing with emotion as he pulls me down onto his knee. "I'll thank God every day for bringing you to me, Lana. You're my miracle, my sweet little star. No one on this earth will love you more fiercely or with more devotion than I do. My heart belongs to you. It beats for you now, and it always will."

"Mine too," I whisper through tears, flinging my arms around his neck again. I bury my face in his throat, clinging to him. "I love you so much, Sawyer."

"I love you, little star." He wraps his arms around me and holds me, his body trembling beneath mine with the weight of what he feels for me. I feel it in the air around us too, seeping into my pores and overfilling my heart. There's an endless well of it, flowing between us like magic.

"This is the best Christmas ever," I whisper.

"This is only the beginning. I have a lifetime of days just like this waiting for you. Christmas will always be magical for you so long as I have a say in it," he says, sliding me back to my feet before he rises to his own. We don't speak again until we're settled in the warm water with his arms around me and my head on his chest.

"I didn't get you anything for Christmas," I murmur then.

"You did," he promises, a smile in his voice. "You gave me back my brother and my family. You gave me your heart. I have everything I need right here." He squeezes me for emphasis. "That's worth more to me than anything you could buy in a store."

"Sawyer," I whisper.

"No more tears, sweet girl. I only ever want to see you smiling." He runs his hand down my arm. "You light up the whole world when you smile at me."

I turn around on his lap, huffing as I slip and slide in all the bubbles, sloshing water over the side of the tub. He catches me around the waist and pulls me up against his chest to keep me from knocking over the tray he set up for us. I wrap my arms around his neck and seek his lips with my own.

"Then light me up, Sawyer," I whisper against his lips. "Make me smile."

"Nah, little star," he breathes, pulling me closer. His hands slip down my body and send heat dancing across my skin. "I'm going to make you shine."

And he does. For a lifetime.

EPILOGUE

SAWYER

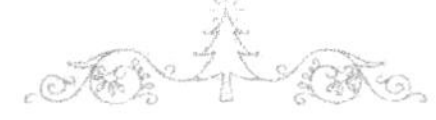

O<u>ne year later</u>

"Sawyer!" Lana cries, breaking my heart. Her face is red and sweaty, her green eyes full of tears. She's so tired, but still so beautiful to me. The last year with her has been the best of my life. She is still the brightest little star I've ever met.

"Breathe, little star," I croon, pressing kisses to her eyelids. "Just keep breathing. You're doing so good."

"I'm so tired," she sobs.

"I know you are, sweet girl." It's Christmas Eve and she's been in labor for over twelve hours already. She needs sleep, but our little girl is as stubborn as her mommy can be.

We're dying to meet her, but she's taking her time making her entrance.

"Just a few more pushes, Lana," Dr. Jola says to my wife, giving her a warm smile. "We're almost there."

"You can do this," I remind her, though I wish I could take the pain for her. I'd carry it without complaint. Even though she's miserable, she's been the sweetest mommy-to-be. Nothing fazes her or gets her down for very long. The first few weeks, she was sick so much. She didn't let it stop her. Hell, she didn't even complain. She's been shining so brightly through the entire pregnancy, ecstatic even over the less fun parts like going pee every five minutes or not being able to sleep comfortably.

I'm in awe of her and her strength. I don't simply love her. I idolize her. She is my fucking hero. My whole world revolves around her. I already know our daughter is going to be just like her. I'm going to lose my mind obsessing about both of them.

I can't wait.

I just hope our little girl is easier to spoil than my wife. She never wants anything, never asks for anything. The simplest gestures light her up. Finding ways to spoil her has been a challenge but I try to rise to the occasion. Sometimes, the Universe throws me an assist like it did this time. Lana said last Christmas was the best ever. I think she might change her mind when she holds our daughter in her arms this Christmas.

"It's time to push again, mama," Dr. Jola says as another contraction begins and Lana groans in pain. "One real big one this time."

"Hold my hand. Squeeze as hard as you need to squeeze," I encourage, helping her get into the proper position to start pushing again.

She latches onto my hand gratefully.

"Push on the count of three," Dr. Jola instructs as the nurses scurry around to help. "One. Two. Three. Push, Lana."

"Push, little star," I murmur, rubbing her back with my free hand.

Her grip on my hand tightens until I'm slightly worried she's going to break it. Her face turns bright red.

"Jack Frost!" she screams at the top of her lungs, pushing through the worst of the contraction.

The entire room goes silent and then one of the nurses laughs quietly before Dr. Jola sends her a sharp glare that has her snapping her mouth closed and standing up straight in an instant. For a woman who looks like someone's favorite grandma and is maybe five feet tall, she's a little terrifying.

"You're doing great, Lana," Dr. Jola says to my wife. "Rest for a minute and then you'll push again one more time."

Lana slumps weakly against the bed, tears trickling down her face. She pants for breath, her sweaty hair stuck to her head.

"You're so beautiful," I whisper, wiping away her tears.

"I l-look terrible."

"No, you look like a mama bear fighting to bring your baby girl into this world," I disagree. "There is nothing more beautiful than that."

"Sawyer," she sobs. "I c-can't do this."

"You can. You've always been stronger than I have." I cup her face in my palm, turning her to face me. Her eyes are dull with pain and full of tears. "From day one, I've been amazed by your strength and courage, by your selflessness and the way you love with your whole heart. Our baby is already so blessed because she has you to look up to. God knows, I am too. So damn blessed."

"Sawyer," she whispers as another round of tears fall down her cheeks.

"No crying, sweet Lana." I glance at the clock and smile. "I promised you that Christmas would always be magical. What's more magical than bringing our baby girl into the world on your favorite day of the year?"

"It's Christmas?" she asks, sniffling.

"It is. You ready to bring our baby home now?"

She sniffles again, trying to get herself under control. And then familiar determination lights those green eyes, and her chin comes up. She looks from me to Dr. Jola. "I'm ready."

"You did so good, little star," I whisper, holding her in my arms while she holds our little girl.

Clara Belle Greenway was born at 12:27am, with hair as blonde as her mommy's. She's as beautiful as my little star too. She came into the world screaming her head off, but as soon as the nurse laid her on Lana's chest, she huffed out a little sigh and stopped crying.

I can't stop staring at the two of them. They're both so fucking perfect. They both shine so brightly. They're my Christmas miracles, so much more than I deserve. I'll spend the rest of my life watching over them, protecting, and loving them.

I've fallen for Lana every single day for the last year but seeing her with my daughter...what I feel for her eclipses love. It's a level of complete adoration that no one has named yet. It's immutable, inviolable, and eternal.

I already love Clara more than I thought it was possible to love one tiny, five-pound human.

"I already love her so much," Lana whispers as if reading my mind. "She's perfect, Sawyer."

"Yeah, she is," I agree, reaching out to touch her little hand. She startles and then her tiny little fist closes around my finger, bringing tears to my eyes. "You're both so damn perfect. Jesus, little star. How'd I get so fucking lucky?"

"It's not luck. It's you." She turns her head, resting her lips against my throat. "You've always been worthy, Sawyer. You're an amazing man, a loving brother, the sweetest principal, and the best husband a woman could ever ask for. I know you're going to be the greatest father too."

"You make me sound like a saint," I say, chuckling.

"Mm, definitely not a saint. You're too dirty for that."

She giggles when I growl at her. I know she isn't complaining though. She's as dirty as I am. We can't seem to keep our hands off one another. Doing it during the week when we're working is close to agony for both of us. We make up for it as soon as we're home. Some days, we don't even make it past the living room before I'm inside her, taking her over and over again.

"It's true," she says. "You are dirty. But you're perfect for me and for Clara. I love you so much, and she already does too. You're going to be her favorite person in the world, just like you're mine."

"Nah, little elf. You'll be her favorite person." I'm not complaining. If I were Clara, I'd choose Lana as my favorite person too. My little star will spoil her with so much love and affection. Being back up for her, being the person she chose to share her life with, the one who gets to help her shine...that's an honor all its own. And being Clara's daddy, being the one who gets to love and protect her while her mommy teaches her to shine too...there's no better feeling in the world than that.

Lana yawns, pressing her face deeper into my throat.

"You should sleep," I murmur. "You've had a long day."

"I don't want to miss a second with her," she says, a pout in her voice. "What if I go to sleep and she does something cute or she cries?"

"She'll do cute things every day of her life," I say, smiling at her. If Clara is anything like her, she'll definitely do cute shit every day. Lana certainly does. "But you have to sleep when she sleeps, or you'll never get any rest. I'll watch over both of you while you sleep."

"You need rest too."

"I'll sleep in a little while. I have to call our parents and Savannah and Saint first. They'll all be mad if I don't." They all wanted to be here, but Lana and I wanted it to be just us in the delivery room. We wanted time with our girl before we share her with the world. Our families will be here tomorrow to meet her and spend Christmas with us. And I already know our moms and Savannah are going to steal Clara as often as possible.

It's going to drive me crazy, but I'll let them do it. Mostly because Lana says I have to share her, but also because I know how excited they all are to meet her. They already love her...a lot if the amount of stuff they've bought her is any indication. She won't have to wear the same outfit basically ever if they keep going at the rate they have been.

With our families around us, our little girl will always know love and safety. As a father, I couldn't ask for anything more for her. Except maybe that she stays little forever so I never have to give her up.

"Merry Christmas," Lana whispers, already drifting off. "I love you."

"Merry Christmas, little star," I whisper back. "I'll love you every day of forever."

"Mmkay," she sighs. "Smart man."

I smile, my heart bursting with joy and my soul full of peace, as she drifts off.

This day—this *moment*—is the best damn Christmas I've ever had. But I know there will be a lifetime more just like it. All because a magical little elf saw something in me worth loving when I wasn't sure how to even love myself. I'll spend the rest of my life thanking God for sending her to me.

She's my Christmas miracle, the best thing that ever happened to me...and I have never felt more worthy than I do with her asleep in my arms with our daughter resting peacefully in hers.

Authors Note

Happy Holidays, lovely. If you enjoyed *His Christmas Miracle*, please consider leaving a review. Reviews are really important for authors like me.

PS: You can download the bonus scene for His Christmas Miracle here.

Savannah and Kieran's story, Taken by the Hitman, and Saint and Everleigh's story, Wicked Saint, are now available!

TAKEN BY THE HITMAN

EXCERPT

"I'm not in my room," I mumble, the first thing that comes to mind. The dorm room I share with Miriam is small, barely big enough for the two of us. This room is triple the size, decorated in dark, masculine colors. The walls are slate gray. The windows are small squares, situated high up on the walls as if to let light in but keep everything else out.

"No," Stranger agrees. He moves suddenly, his face looming into view.

I instinctively rear backward before I can stop myself.

He notices.

"I'm not going to hurt you, little one," he murmurs.

"You just killed a man."

His jaw hardens. So do his eyes. "No. I killed a piece of shit parading as a man," he says. Despite the lethality in his expression, his voice is soft. Is he trying to soothe me? How strange. "Jack Stinson didn't deserve to live."

He's not wrong about that. Still....

"Am I your prisoner now?"

This startles him.

"You think I'm going to keep you against your will?"

I shrug, not sure what I think. "Isn't there a rule against people like you leaving witnesses alive?" I'd much rather be his prisoner than be dead. At least as a prisoner, there's a chance of escape. Dead is dead no matter how you slice it.

I'm not afraid of this man though. It's bizarre, but I've felt completely safe with him almost since I set eyes on him. He's a fascinating combination of light and dark, and I find myself...drawn to him. My therapist told me once that people who survive a crisis together tend to forge bonds with one another because they share an experience few others understand. I don't think this is that though. I don't think it's Stockholm Syndrome either. Being around him just feels...right, as insane as that sounds.

"I'm not going to hurt you, little one," he says again. "You're safe with me. And you aren't a prisoner either. I simply didn't know where to take you after you fainted, so I brought you here."

"Oh," I whisper, my cheeks heating at the reminder that I fainted...and in embarrassment for accusing him of kidnapping me. He may be a killer, but he's been nothing but nice to me. I push myself into a sitting position. "Where exactly is here?"

"A safehouse."

"Oh." That tells me absolutely nothing. His safehouse could be in Bora Bora for all I know.

"We're still in the city, Savannah," he says, his lips twitching.

Am I that easy to read?

I narrow my eyes on him. He said my name before, but it didn't register. "You know my name."

"I do."

"Will you tell me yours?"

"People call me Ghost."

"Ghost," I repeat and then smile. "You don't seem very specter-like to me."

"That's because you aren't most people." His eyes run over me, searching for something. I'm not sure what, exactly. He seems frustrated when he doesn't find whatever it is. "How old are you?"

"Eighteen. Do you kill people often?"

"As often as it needs doing."

"For money?"

"Among other things," he says.

I process that for a moment and then sigh. "Okay."

"Okay?" That brow arches upward again.

"Would you prefer I faint again?" I ask, which makes his lip twitch as if he wants to laugh again. I'm making a hitman laugh. A ridiculously hot hitman. Awesome.

Why am I not freaking out right now?

"Kieran."

"Kieran?"

"You call me Kieran, not Ghost."

"Oh." Wow. I think he just told me his real name. I'm guessing that's not something he does very often. He wouldn't make a very good hitman if he did, would he? "How did you know about Jack?"

"My boss gave me the intel."

"You have a boss?"

"Yes."

"Wow. Hitmanning is way more organized than I expected."

"Hitmanning?" His lips twitch again.

"You know what I mean," I say, waving a hand in the air. "I'm not exactly familiar with the lingo here. Until tonight, I thought hitmen existed only in action movies and the CIA." I press my hands to my cheeks as if that's going to cool me down or halt the endless circles in my mind. "You don't work for the CIA, do you?"

"No."

"I didn't think so."

"You're handling this well," he observes, searching my face again.

"I passed out."

"You didn't scream."

"You told me not to scream."

"Do you always do what you're told?"

"You had a gun." I never do what I'm told, especially if Saint or Sawyer is the one trying to boss me around. I'm not telling him that though. "Following your orders seemed like the safest thing to do."

"You're not like most girls, are you?"

"Am so," I lie.

He notices. I get a genuine smile this time. It doesn't look natural on him, but it softens him a little, makes him seem less like a mythical warrior and more human. My stomach flutters as butterflies kick into flight. I shiver even though I'm not cold. He's warming me up in places he shouldn't again.

TAKEN BY THE HITMAN IS NOW AVAILABLE.

NICHOLE'S BOOK BEAUTIES

Want to connect with Nichole and other readers? We're building a girl gang! Join Nichole Rose's Book Beauties on Facebook for fun, games, and behind-the-scenes exclusives!

INSTALOVE BOOK CLUB

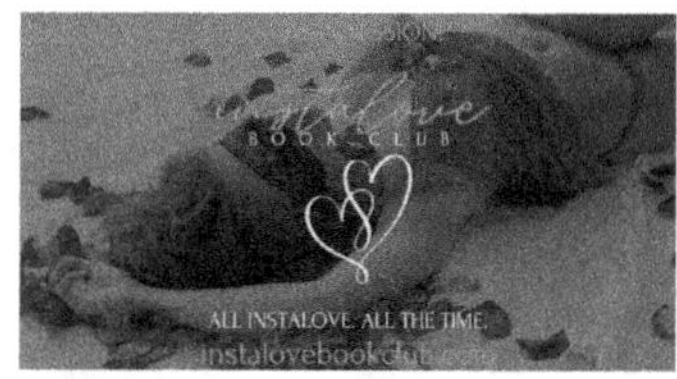

The Instalove Book Club is now in session!

Get the inside scoop from your favorite instalove authors, meet new authors to love, and snag freebies and bonus content from featured authors every month. The Instalove Book Club newsletter goes out once per week!

Join now to get your hands on bonus scenes and brand-new, exclusive content from our first six featured authors.

Join the Club: http://instalovebookclub.com

FOLLOW NICHOLE

Sign-up for Nichole's mailing list at http://authorni cholerose.com/newsletter to stay up to date on all new releases and for exclusive ARC giveaways from Nichole Rose.

Want to connect with Nichole and other readers? Join Nichole Rose's Book Beauties on Facebook!

facebook.com/AuthorNicholeRose/

instagram.com/AuthorNicholeRose

twitter.com/AuthNicholeRose

bookbub.com/authors/nichole-rose

tiktok.com/@authornicholerose

MORE BY NICHOLE ROSE

<u>Her Alpha Series</u>

Her Alpha Daddy Next Door

Her Alpha Boss Undercover

Her Alpha's Secret Baby

Her Alpha Protector

Her Date with an Alpha

Her Alpha: The Complete Series

<u>Her Bride Series</u>

His Future Bride

His Stolen Bride

His Secret Bride

His Curvy Bride

His Captive Bride

His Blushing Bride

His Bride: The Complete Series

Claimed Series

Possessing Liberty

Teaching Rowan

Claiming Caroline

Kissing Kennedy

Claimed: The Complete Series

Love on the Clock Series

Adore You

Hold You

Keep You

Protect You

Love on the Clock: The Complete Series

The Billionaires' Club

The Billionaire's Big Bold Weakness

The Billionaire's Big Bold Wish

The Billionaire's Big Bold Woman

The Billionaire's Big Bold Wonder

Playing for Keeps

Cutie Pie

Ice Breaker

Ice Prince

Ice Giant

The Second Generation

A Blushing Bride for Christmas

Love Bites

Come Undone

Dripping Pearls

Silver Spoon MC

The Surgeon

The Heir

The Lawyer

The Prodigy

The Bodyguard

Silver Spoon MC Collection: Nichole's Crew

Echoes of Forever

His Christmas Miracle

Taken by the Hitman

Wicked Saint

The Ruined Trilogy

Physical Science

Wrecked

Wanton

Destination Romance

Romancing the Cowboy

Beach House Beauty

Standalone Titles

A Touch of Summer

Black Velvet

His Secret Obsession

Dirty Boy

Naughty Little Elf

Tempted by December

Devil's Deceit

A Bride for the Beast (writing with Fern Fraser)

A Hero for Her

<u>Easy on Me</u>
Easy Ride
Easy Surrender

<u>One Night with You</u>
Falling Hard
Model Behavior
Learning Curve
Angel Kisses

<u>Silver Spoon Falls</u>
Xavier's Kitten
Callum's Hope
Snow's Prince
Aurora's Knight (coming soon)

<u>writing with Loni Ree as Loni Nichole</u>
Dillon's Heart
Razor's Flame
Ryker's Reward
Zane's Rebel

Oral Arguments

Grizz's Passion (coming soon)

ABOUT NICHOLE ROSE

Nichole Rose is a short romance author on the west coast. Her books feature headstrong, sassy women and the alpha males who consume them. From grumpy detectives to country boys with attitude to instalove and over-the-top declarations, nothing is off-limits.

Nichole is sure to have a steamy, sweet story just right for everyone. She fully believes the world is ugly enough without trying to fit falling in love into a one-size-fits-all box. When not writing, Nichole enjoys fine wine, cute shoes, and everything supernatural. She is happily married to the love of her life and is a proud mama to the world's most ridiculous fur-babies.

You can learn more about Nichole and her books at authornicholerose.com.

facebook.com/AuthorNicholeRose/

instagram.com/AuthorNicholeRose

twitter.com/AuthNicholeRose

bookbub.com/authors/nichole-rose

tiktok.com/@authornicholerose